ALIEN SUPERSTAR

BY HENRY WINKLER AND LIN OLIVER

ILLUSTRATED BY ETHAN NICOLLE

Amulet Books

New York

Library of Congress Cataloging-in-Publication Data
Names: Winkler, Henry, 1945- author. | Oliver, Lin, author.
Title: Alien superstar / Henry Winkler and Lin Oliver.
Description: New York: Amulet Books, 2019. | Summary: Buddy Burger escapes his home planet, lands in Hollywood, and is cast in a new television series, but must pretend his six eyes and suction-cup feet are the costume and his human skin, real.
Identifiers: LCCN 2019000754 | ISBN 9781419733697 (alk. paper)
Subjects: | CYAC: Extraterrestrial beings—Fiction. | Disguise—Fiction. | Actors and actresses—Fiction. | Television programs—Production and direction—Fiction. | Humorous stories.
Classification: LCC PZ7.W72934 Ah 2019 | DDC [Fic]—dc23

B&N edition ISBN 978-1-4197-4528-7
Text copyright © 2019 Henry Winkler and Lin Oliver
Illustrations copyright © 2019 Ethan Nicolle
Book design by Hana Anouk Nakamura and Chad W. Beckerman

Printed and bound in U.S.A.

10 9 8 7 6 5 4 3 2

ABRAMS The Art of Books
195 Broadway, New York, NY 10007
abramsbooks.com

1

This was no way to celebrate a birthday.

I could hear the breath escaping from my third lung, the one that kicks into gear when I'm terrified. The red dust that covers my planet clouded my eyes—all six of them. But there was no time to unscrew them and soak them in fermented beetle legs, which as I'm sure you know is the only way to clean intergalactic dust off your retinas. The Squadron was gaining on me. I could feel the heat of their laser beams nipping at the suction cups that cover the bottom of my feet.

Run, I thought to myself, *like your life depends on it*.

Which it did.

"Citizen Short Nose," one of the Squadron commanders yelled. "Stop immediately. There is no escape for you."

"Don't you dare stop, Grandson Short Nose," my grandmother said, panting. I could hear the exhaustion in her voice. Being chased by the deadliest assault squadron in the galaxy is not easy when you're 987 years old.

I glanced out of my two rear eyes and saw my grandmother falling behind. My sensory enhancer, the trunk-like appendage that grows out of my upper back, must have smelled her fear. It's good at that, just like it's good at enhancing all our other senses like taste, touch, sight, and hearing. Instinctively, my enhancer stretched out to grab my grandmother's hand. She slapped it away, and I felt the sting reverberate through my body.

"Don't help me, Grandson Short Nose!" she wheezed with her last bit of energy. "Escape from here and meet your destiny."

"I can't leave you, grandmother Wrinkle."

"This is our plan, grandson. My life is nearing its end. Yours is just beginning."

Those were the last words I heard her say as the Squadron threw a titanium net over her frail body.

"We have the old one," the commander shouted. "Surrender now and you both will survive."

Survival was not my goal. *Living* was. There was no way I could live my life if I stayed here. They would neutralize me. Deactivate my sensory enhancer. Eliminate my ability to experience all the wonders of life. Turn me into one of them—robotic, joyless, dead. No. I couldn't. I wouldn't.

I summoned the strength to run even faster, forcing myself not to look back. The red sun was setting, and I had to be at the Cemetery before the moonrise was complete or I would never be able to break out of my planet's gravitational pull. But my stupid suction cups were not helping me. Here's a piece of advice for you—if you need to get somewhere fast, remove all suction cups from your feet.

Unfortunately, I couldn't. I was born with them.

The Squadron was gaining on me. I could see Red Algae Ravine just ahead. The Cemetery was at the bottom, down a steep winding road. I made an instant and dangerous decision.

Closing all six of my eyes, grabbing my sensory enhancer and pulling it close to my body, I tucked into a ball and flung myself off the rim of the ravine. I hit the ground hard and hurtled down the canyon, bouncing off jagged rocks that punctured my outer epidermal layer, what you humans call "skin." The pain was so intense I couldn't even scream.

Just when I thought I couldn't bear it anymore, I hit bottom and crashed headfirst into the iron wall that surrounded the Cemetery. My head was spinning, but there was no time for dizzy. Half the Squadron were up on the rim, firing laser beams at me, while the other half were scrambling down the road, also taking shots at me. I staggered to my feet and made my way to the secret keypad buried in a hidden compartment of the wall. Grandmother Wrinkle had instructed me to memorize the code, but now my mind was blank.

I was codeless.

"Stop!"

The commander's voice was near. I couldn't tell exactly how close it was, but I knew it was too close.

"Don't be a fool! Give yourself up!" he bellowed.

The code! The code!

It was right there in my memory, but clouded by fear. Grandmother picked it because it was my favorite character from all the Earth movies we secretly watched together.

Of course.

With my fingers trembling, I reached out and punched in S-K-Y-W-A-L-K-E-R.

The heavy gate rumbled open. I slipped through and pressed the button on the other side to close it.

Wait! Was that a hand I saw, reaching through the gate, trying to grab me? The piercing scream I heard as the gate slammed shut confirmed my suspicion.

The Cemetery was the final resting place for our planet's obsolete vehicles. My grandmother would often go there to gather spare parts for old spaceships that she repaired. Because she had been the best master mechanic in the fleet, she knew every piece of equipment that was there, and had even secretly changed the code that opened the gate. Over the last year, she had snuck me in every afternoon, to prepare for this very moment when I would escape the fate that was awaiting me. She remembered a time before the New Squadron, when life on our planet was colorful and creative and fragrant, and her fervent wish was that I would have that life too.

I knew every object in the Cemetery as well as my grandmother did. They were like old friends. I dodged my way across rusted-out spacecraft, forging a path through shattered interstellar fighters, busted-up afterburners, and an assortment of broken wings.

"Citizen Short Nose," the Squadron commander shouted, using the vocal cord amplifier built into his neck. "We have you trapped. You've given yourself no way out."

That's what you think, you robotic puppet of the state, I thought.

I ducked behind the mountain of broken wings and pulled the metallic tarp off the faster-than-light vehicle Grandmother Wrinkle and I had rebuilt for my escape. There it was—but would it actually fly? We never had the opportunity to test it. As I climbed the ladder to the hatch, I felt a searing pain in my arm. My front eyes saw purple blood spurt from my shoulder as my rear eyes detected the soldier who had scaled the wall and shot me.

Clutching my shoulder, I jumped into the vehicle and slid into the driver's seat. I buckled myself in with my good arm and pulled the hatch closed, when suddenly it flew open again. My sensory enhancer had sprung into action and was pushing the door open every time I tried to close it.

"Oh no! Not now!" I groaned.

It snorted fiendishly. I knew that snort. It was reserved for only the most delicious of aromas.

I looked through the open hatch and saw what the attraction was. A single vine of honeywort had pushed through the pile of broken wings, stretching its orange blossom up into the atmosphere. My sensory enhancer was going wild from the sweet floral fragrance. I was going wild from the constant ping of laser shots bouncing off the open hatch. Those shots were coming from close range. The Squadron was closing in.

I reached out and grabbed my sensory enhancer, which had wrapped itself around the vine and was making deep grunting sounds as it inhaled the honeywort blossom. I yanked it inside with a vengeance and slammed the hatch shut.

"Your timing sucks," I screamed at it, pulling the orange blossom from its trunk. "For once, do as I say."

In the human world, I know you don't make it a practice of yelling at your body parts. But sensory enhancers can have a mind of their own. They respond to all stimuli. That's what is both wonderful and tricky about them—and that's what makes them dangerous.

I pressed the ignition and the panel lit up, showing my destination coordinates. That was a good sign. Fighting through the pain in my arm, I grabbed the accelerator and pushed it forward. The entire vehicle shuddered but did not lift off. I heard a pounding on the window and turned to see the commander's face, pressed against the glass.

"Surrender!" he shouted.

"Never, creepoid!"

"Every thirteen-year-old on this planet goes through it," the commander snarled. "Once your sensory enhancer is deactivated, you won't miss it."

"I refuse to become like you, one of the living dead."

I reached for the altitude lever, but I couldn't get a tight grip. My own blood had soaked my glove, making the lever slippery.

It was now or never. This was my last chance.

I grabbed the lever with both hands and pushed it forward with all my   might. I heard it engage and felt the vehicle lift off the   ground, slowly gaining altitude.

The commander was hanging on to the wing, barking at me to land the craft. Ignoring him, I activated the particle accelerator and we shot forward, heading at breakneck speed toward the wall of the Cemetery. I needed lift. Immediately, if not sooner.

I located the thruster switches on both sides of the driver's seat and pushed them down as far as they would go. The nose of the vehicle turned upward. The sudden burst of velocity made the commander lose his grip. From my rear eyes, I saw him plummet through the air, heading toward a pile of jagged metal refuse far below.

My vehicle shot up over the rim of the ravine. I looked out the window and saw that the moon had just reached its highest point. I had been seconds away from total failure.

The red dwarf sun faded into the distance and the vastness of space lay before me.

As we hit maximum velocity and barreled into the galaxy, the g-force pushed me against my seat, compressing all my internal organs. My stomach flattened and my bodily gases exploded out of me. They erupted with such force that I was pretty sure my vehicle picked up speed. My body rumbled with a thunderous noise. On Earth, I believe you call that a giant fart.

That was the last thing I remember before I passed out.

2

When I came to, I had no idea where I was or how much time had elapsed. Grandma Wrinkle had preprogrammed my vehicle to land on planet Earth, but I couldn't tell how far along in the journey I was. I swiveled all six of my eyes to the front and looked out the windshield at the panoramic view. *Wow, space is beautiful*, I thought as I surveyed the swirling misty spiral ahead of me filled with two hundred billion stars. Moving my eyes to the left side of my head, I noticed a shimmering yellow planet circled by glowing rings of brown, gray, and pink.

Wait a minute! That misty spiral had to be the Milky Way, and the glowing planet was Saturn. That meant I was only 746 million miles from Earth, give or take 50 million! I realize that to you this might seem far, but then you humans are still driving around on four rubber tires surrounded by steel. I don't want to make you feel bad, but where I come from, our technology is way beyond that. Without getting into the physics of it, let's just say my faster-than-light vehicle was using teleportation to get me to Earth in less time than it would take you guys to drive from Big Arm, Montana, to Green Acres, North Dakota.

I suddenly became aware of a gnawing feeling in my stomach and remembered Grandma Wrinkle's warning.

"I have left some nutrient wafers for you in the sustenance box in the dashboard," she had said. "I couldn't leave more because every ounce counts and I didn't want to weigh down your vehicle. The wafers will provide the nourishment you need until you figure out what will sustain you on Earth. And remember, you must always drink lots of water to maintain your life force."

As I reached out to open the sustenance box, I felt a burning sting in my shoulder. All my eyes raced to the right side of my head and glanced down at the wound, which was already scabbing over with dark purple blood. The pressurization system Grandma Wrinkle had installed inside my vehicle was healing the wound faster than normal. I hoped it would be entirely healed by the time I landed on Earth. It's hard to make a good first impression when you have fresh purple blood gushing out of your body.

I took out one of the wafers and popped it in my mouth. Immediately, I felt a burst of energy as it dissolved on my tongue. There was no need to chew—our species evolved past teeth eons ago. That must sound pretty good to you earthlings, who still have to go to the dentist every year. I hear they drill holes in your teeth, which doesn't sound like a lot of fun.

Our Supreme Leader had decreed that our nutrient wafers should have every speck of taste baked out of them so that our senses are never stimulated. He believes that stimulated senses can lead to all kinds of trouble, as if enjoying a pepperoni pizza is the first step to overthrowing a repressive government.

Even though I could have eaten all the wafers at once, I forced myself to leave one behind until I figured out what kind of Earth food I could eat. Earth food looked great in the movies and television shows Grandma Wrinkle and I watched secretly in her underground cellar. Especially ice cream. It looked like such fun to use your tongue as a spoon. Or spaghetti, which looks like a huge pile of string.

Does it tie itself in knots in your stomach? I wondered.

Suddenly, a massive object appeared, zooming right toward me.

"Evade! Evade!" I screamed, with only me there to hear it.

I grabbed the altitude lever and pulled, forcing my

vehicle to shoot up and over the object. As it whizzed past, I looked down and realized it was a satellite with the gigantic letters *USA* emblazoned on its solar panels. That meant I must be close to Earth. Looking out the windshield, I could see the circular curve of the blue planet come into view. My three lungs started to work overtime, inhaling gulps of air in a combination of excitement and fear.

There it was. Earth.

I was heading right to the spot Grandma Wrinkle had programmed, our favorite address on Earth, the one we saw at the end of so many movies.

Universal Studios, North Hollywood, California.

We were the only ones on our planet who even knew movies existed. Grandma Wrinkle had remembered seeing several as a child at the Great Library, before it was destroyed by the new government, and she never forgot the influence they'd had on her. Later, being the master engineer that she is, she invented a device to funnel earthly movies and television across the universe directly to her cellar. We watched those movies endlessly, laughing and crying over every detail. And that's how I learned that creativity had to always be in my life. I couldn't be me without it.

Had our Supreme Leader or any of the Squadron discovered Grandma Wrinkle's cache of entertainment, she would have been placed in a single-being prison capsule and shot into space, banished forever. And I wouldn't have been far behind. But our dream was that if I could reach Universal Studios before my sensory enhancer was deactivated, I would be safe and able to live my life as I knew it needed to be lived.

"Landing coordinates in range." The monotone voice of the onboard computer startled me.

"Repeat, please," I said.

"Landing coordinates are locked in. Are you prepared?"

"Yes." I gulped. I wasn't sure if I was at all prepared, but when you're billions of miles from home, you want to let the universe know you're confident, even if you're not.

"Make sure you go to the bathroom before you land," the computer droned.

"What am I, a baby?" I snapped.

BABIES ARE DEFINED AS ONE YEAR OR YOUNGER. YOU ARE THIRTEEN,

SO THE ANSWER IS NO.

"Babies are defined as one year or younger. You are thirteen, so the answer is no."

Computers have no sense of humor. That's the same no matter what planet you live on.

The ride got very bumpy as we drew near Earth. My sensory enhancer burrowed closer to my body and hid in my armpit, obviously reacting to the change in atmosphere. I heard it take a whiff and then let out a big grunt. I couldn't blame it—I hadn't washed in days. I wrapped my fingers around the armrest until all fourteen of my knuckles turned white. Looking out the window, I could make out an ocean and a coastline, giving way to ribbons of highways packed with adorable little vehicles. There they were, four rubber tires surrounded by steel.

I heard the braking system engage and felt the landing legs descend from the belly of my spaceship. The pull of Earth's gravity and the drag from its atmosphere slowed us down enough for a gentle approach. Looking out the window, I saw a crowd of humanoids looking up at the sky— real, live, actual human beings that I had only seen in movies or television. But these humans were wearing big hats and flowered shirts of all different colors. On my planet, you could go to prison for wearing clothes like that.

As my ship hovered above the crowd, the heat and

downdraft sent the people running for cover, scattering like colossal red sand beetles do when asteroids collide. You know how that is.

At first, the humans looked frightened, and I couldn't blame them. It's probably not every day that you see a spaceship land right in front of your eyes, even during tours at Universal Studios, where people come to see movie magic like fake shark attacks and wizard castles and giant mechanical apes with banana breath.

The ship shuddered and touched down with a thud. I looked out the window and stared at the crowd of people. What I saw was them staring back at me. Not one eye was blinking. Not one mouth was moving. Not one hand was waving.

Would these people welcome an alien? Or would I be attacked and have to lock myself inside this capsule for the rest of my life?

I unbuckled my seat belt, filled my three lungs with air, and reached for the door handle.

There was no turning back.

3

As I pushed open the door, the first thing that struck me was the sun. I mean it literally struck me, shooting bright yellow beams into every one of my eyes. Living on a red dwarf planet, the light is always dim. The bright light of Earth was unbearable.

I quickly retreated back into my vehicle and reached into the drawer where Grandma Wrinkle had placed emergency supplies like ointments, lotions, and a nail clipper. We have to clip our fingernails twice a day unless we're planning to use them as a personal back scratcher. I shuffled the contents of the drawer until I found what I was looking for.

Sunglasses.

Well, you might not call them sunglasses. They're actually tinted monocles, single lenses that clip on to each eye. As I snapped them into place, which by the way does not hurt, I realized that one was missing. I rummaged around the drawer some more, until I was interrupted by a loud pounding on the exit hatch.

"Come out!" the muffled voices called. I looked out the window and saw a crowd of humans gathering around me. "We want to take selfies!"

Selfies? What was that? I thought I knew English. I've been taught seventy-two languages, and I'm fluent in seventy-one. Hungarian still gives me problems. But I had never heard the word "selfie" before. My brain ran through my Earth dictionary searching for the word, but it came up empty. The closest I got was "self": *that which distinguishes us from another person.* I did have a self, but I wasn't about to give that away.

The pounding on the hatch was becoming more urgent.

"We don't have all day," yelled a man with a colorful fire-breathing dragon on his arm. "We have to get to Harry Potter World before lunch. Open the door!"

No wonder he's in such a rush, I thought. *I would be too if I had a fire-breathing dragon burning my upper arm.* I still couldn't find the missing monocle, so my only choice was to shut my sixth eye and move it to the back of my head. Even though I was toothless, I plastered the biggest smile I could muster on my face, hoping that my bright red gums would not freak the humans out. I opened the hatch to meet these creatures I only knew from movies and television.

As soon as the door swung open and I stuck my head out, the whole crowd burst into applause.

"That's one heck of a costume!" a large man with hairy arms said. Then he grabbed me around the shoulders and shoved his face in close to mine.

"Smile for Auntie Bertha back in Minnesota," he said, holding me so hard I thought my neck was going to get a permanent crick in it.

Then he snapped a picture with his cell phone. I had seen one of those phones in a museum on my planet, from

when they were used eons ago. Now, of course, they're obsolete, because we can take a picture out of any of our six eyes.

The man held up the phone and showed the picture to everyone.

"Aunt Bertha's false teeth are going to drop right out of her mouth when she sees me with googly-eyes here."

No one had ever called my eyes googly before. I felt a twinge of sadness. I really was far from home. A few tears formed in eyes three, four, and five, which are the ones with the biggest tear ducts. The tears made it hard to see, especially because my sixth eye was still closed against the searing California sunlight.

I searched the crowd. The first thing I saw was a small child with a bright blue tongue wearing a shirt that said LIFE IS BETTER WITH MAC & CHEESE. She was drinking an icy blue substance through a straw that stuck out from a round plastic lid.

"Can I borrow that lid?" I asked her. "I really need it."

"Watch, everybody!" she giggled, handing me the lid. "That alien's probably going to eat this plastic lid for lunch."

I swiveled my sixth eye around to the front, took the lid from the girl's hand, and popped it onto my eyeball. It blocked out almost all the sun, and my eye felt so much better. What didn't feel better was my sensory enhancer. I could feel it coming to life, and I had no idea which of all the sights and sounds and smells in front of me was stimulating it. I didn't have to wait long to find out. Suddenly, it shot straight up in the air and started to sniff and search. It seemed to be focusing on the blue substance in the cup the girl was holding.

"Oh no!" I said to it. "Don't you dare!"

But as you know by now, sensory enhancers have a mind of their own, and the aroma of the icy substance was irresistible to its smell receptors. Making a wild snuffling sound, it dove into the blue slushie, splashing it all over the girl's mac & cheese tee shirt.

"Whoa, will you look at that thing attached to the alien's back," a boy with metal on his teeth yelled. "That's the best special effect I've ever seen!"

That took a lot of nerve, coming from a kid whose metal teeth flashed in the sun like a blinking lightbulb.

People starting snapping pictures as my sensory enhancer continued to twirl wildly in the air, inhaling the blue slushie and spraying it across the whole crowd. I thought that would make them angry, but they all laughed and cheered. These humans have a great sense of humor.

"He likes the blue raspberry flavor just like me," a little boy sitting on his father's shoulders shouted. "I love you, creature!"

A word of advice to you earthlings. You should never talk to a sensory enhancer when it's on a sniffing binge. Mine turned to the little boy and squirted a big glob of blue slush right at him. The boy laughed uncontrollably and my sensory enhancer joined in, squealing with a pitch so high my ears started to vibrate. Then it flopped on top of the boy's head and nuzzled his forehead, just as the boy's mother captured it all on her phone.

"Look at that!" the kid with the shiny teeth shouted. "That thing just photobombed the lady's video."

"Who ever thought you'd be the star of the show today, Leo?" the boy's mother said. "I'll bet this video gets tons of views. You'll be our family's first movie star."

The crowd moved in so close and so intensely that even with my third lung it was hard to breathe. I couldn't get away from them—there was nowhere for me to go. I couldn't push through the crowd, and the hatch behind me was closed. I was stuck, and I started to feel the same terror I felt when the Squadron was chasing me.

From out of nowhere, a large rubbery green hand grabbed my wrist. I tried to escape its strong grasp and climb up the side of my vehicle, but I couldn't move because it was holding me so tightly. I looked up to see that my wrist was being held by a tall monster towering above the crowd.

His horrible green head was attached to his neck with metal bolts. He lurched forward at me and snarled.

Oh, this is great, I thought. *I've only been on Earth for three minutes and already I'm going to die.*

"Come with me, buddy," the monster said. That kind voice did not sound like it should come from that face.

"Over here, Frankenstein," the man with the hairy arms shouted, holding his phone in the air. "Give me one of your monster smiles."

"Not now, dude," the monster said. "Spaceman and I are going on lunch break. We'll be back at two."

"We will?" I squeaked.

"Let's blow this pop stand," Frankenstein answered. "I got a meatloaf sandwich waiting in the break room."

Frankenstein tugged on my arm, but once again, I couldn't move, this time because the suction cups on the bottom of my feet were stuck solidly to the ground. The pavement was hot and the heat must have made the suction even stronger.

"You coming or what?" Frankenstein asked.

"I'd like to, but I seem to have a suction cup problem."

He reached out and put his green hands under each of my armpits and lifted me straight up in the air. I could hear the suction cups pop as they let go of the pavement. He pointed to my sensory enhancer.

"You taking that thing with you?" he asked.

"Yes I am. It's attached."

"Wow, these costumes are getting better every day," he said.

Carrying me under his arm like a bag of asteroid fragments, he edged his way through the crowd, saying, "Coming through, folks. Lunch break."

Even though they continued to snap pictures, people cleared a path for us and we were able to make our way to a road where a tram full of tourists was rolling by. A tour guide spoke into a microphone.

"Over there is the pond where the famous mechanical shark from *Jaws* lives," the tour guide droned. "Keep your hands in the vehicle, folks. That fish loves to nibble on tourists from the Midwest. And, whoa, look at that. We're in luck. There's Frankenstein, the iconic film monster first made famous by Boris Karloff in 1931. Not to gross you out, but Frankenstein was created from body parts of deceased people."

"You're deceased, as in dead?" I said to the monster. "Funny, you don't smell like you're rotting."

"What's with you, buddy? We both know this is a rubber suit. Now smile, the park guests are taking pictures."

I looked up at the tram and everyone was standing, holding up their phones. I flashed them my smile.

"Cool!" someone yelled. "The alien has red gums. What's his name?"

"Actually, I've never seen him before," the tour guide said. "Maybe he's a character in a new show. That's Hollywood for you, folks . . . Something new every day."

The tram pulled away.

"The break room is right over there by the dinosaur ride." Frankenstein pointed a large green finger to a bungalow that was hidden behind a jungle landscape. "Think you can manage if I put you down?"

"I think so."

"Okay, just watch out for dinosaur dung."

"You still have dinosaurs here?"

"Nah. I'm just pulling your suction cup."

He put me down, and I started walking on my tiptoes, which seemed to keep the suction cups from sticking to the ground. We headed toward the bungalow, passing a stand that sold a twisted brown thing covered in what looked like little crystals of sodium chloride. The sign above the stand said PRETZELS.

"Those are interesting," I said. "Do you wear them as decoration?"

"Yeah, a lot of people wear them as bracelets," Frankenstein said with a chuckle. "Works out great, because if they get hungry, they got a snack right there on their wrist. And when you slather one of those puppies in mustard, can't beat it."

"I slathered myself in mustard once," I said, trying to sound like I knew what I was talking about. "It kept me really cool."

"You are definitely strange, buddy."

"Oh, you have no idea."

"By the way, I don't think I caught your name," Frankenstein said. "Mine's Luis Rivera."

"But I thought your name was Frankenstein."

"Listen, buddy, you can drop the act now. You don't have to be an alien twenty-four seven. Cut the act and just tell me your name."

"On my planet, they call me Citizen Short Nose."

"Man, you are really into this," Luis sighed.

"My birth name is XR 23 Zeta 5466."

"This is getting annoying," Luis said, "so let me be clear. I'm asking what your Earth name is, because that happens to be the planet we're living on."

Grandma Wrinkle and I hadn't completely thought this through. In our haste to get me off my home planet, we didn't have time to pick an Earth name for me, and I needed it now. The big green guy had stopped walking and was just staring at me. My mind was spinning.

"It's not a hard question, buddy," Luis said.

Buddy. There it was.

"That's my name. Buddy."

"And do you happen to have a last name, or is that also too hard a question?"

Actually, it was a hard question. I glanced around in desperation, using all six eyes to survey my surroundings for an idea.

"Awesome," Luis said. "Your costume's automated. You have a remote control for your eyes?"

Two of my eyes had stopped at a particularly busy food stand. The sign above it said CHEESEBURGERS—THE BEST ON THE BACK LOT.

"Cheeseburger," I said to Luis. "My last name is Cheeseburger."

"What kind of nutty family do you have, naming you after a fast food?"

Obviously, I had put my foot in my mouth, suction cups and all.

"Well, cheese is actually my middle name," I backtracked. "Mostly I just use the initial C. Buddy C. Burger."

"Okay, that's slightly less nutty," Luis said. "One day, I'd like to meet your parents and have a conversation. But now I'm starving. So come on, Buddy C. Burger, let's get us some meatloaf."

He threw his big green arm around my shoulder and we headed to the break room. Just like that, I had a name and my first Earth friend.

4

When we walked into the employee break room, I couldn't believe any of my eyes. Everyone there was half-human, half-creature. There was a man with the body of a raptor but a humanoid face. A woman with blond hair had the furry body of an orange-and-black tiger. And there were two huge ogres, a male and a female, both enjoying green salads with no tomatoes while laughing with their mouths full.

"These are some very unusual humans," I whispered to Luis.

"It's a good crew," he said. "Everyone in here is a wannabe actor and we're just doing this, strolling around in costumes posing for pictures, while we're waiting for our big break."

"Does anyone doing this ever become a star?"

"Sometimes. My best friend, Paul, went from being Puddles Panda Bear to hosting *Covered in Slime*, the messiest game show on TV."

I couldn't believe it. Here I was on Earth, hanging out with real live actors and messy game show hosts.

"Hey, everyone, meet the new kid on the block," Luis said as we walked in. "This is Buddy C. Burger. Buddy, this is everyone."

"What's up, Buddy?" one of the ogres said to me.

"Well, the ceiling is up," I answered. "And if you go farther, you've got the sky, and beyond that is the Milky Way, followed by the entire intergalactic system."

"I wasn't asking for a science lesson," the ogre said. "I was just curious about how you're feeling."

"Ohhhhh. I'm happy to be here."

"I got to get this head off," Luis told me. "It feels like a sauna in here."

To my utter surprise, Luis reached up and pulled off his entire Frankenstein head. Underneath, he was human, just like everyone else in the room. I let out a shriek.

"Why don't you take your costume off too, Buddy?" Luis asked. "Relax. We're on break."

"Um . . . Thanks anyway," I stammered, "but I think I'll just leave it on. This costume is really hard to get back into. You know, it's so skintight I almost feel like it's a part of me."

"Yeah, I like to keep my costume on too," the man dressed as a raptor said. "Comes in handy. I can open a soda can with my big-toe claw."

"Speaking of which," Luis said, "I'm getting a cold drink. Want one, Buddy?"

I suddenly became aware of a tremendous thirst that had overtaken my body, making me feel weak and shaky.

"I could really use something to drink," I answered.

Luis went over to a machine and dropped in some silver coins and a can of liquid rolled out. I had seen a vending machine in the movies, but it was exciting to see one right in front of me.

"Here, let me open that for you," the man in the raptor suit said. He took the can from Luis, popped the top with his toe claw, and handed it over to me. When I took a swig, my whole face felt like it was being attacked by bubbles. I rubbed my nose as hard as I could to get rid of the fizzy sensation, but when I opened my mouth, out came a long, loud burp. I knew what that was because I had seen people burp in the movies. Once, I even saw an actor who could say a whole sentence while burping.

Everyone in the break room laughed at my burp.

"Nice one," the tiger woman commented.

"Why thank you." I smiled.

Luis went to his locker and came back carrying a metal lunch box with a picture of a guy in a leather jacket sitting on a motorcycle.

"Hey, I know that guy," I said. "I saw him on a show called *Happy Days*."

"Dude, you weren't even born when that show was on," Luis said.

"Grandma Wrinkle showed me the videos. It was her favorite show."

"Wait a minute," Luis said as he pulled up a chair and sat down at the table. "You call your grandmother Wrinkle? That's rude, dude. That would be like me calling my grandmother Grandma Bunion."

Everybody in the room laughed, but I didn't know why. My brain ran through my entire Earth dictionary, and the only "bunion" I found was defined as *a bulging bump on the base of your big toe*.

"I'm so sorry about your grandmother's bulging toe," I said to Luis.

He put his hand on my shoulder. "Buddy boy, here's how bunion is spelled. J-O-K-E."

Oh, that word I knew right away. Joke: *something that's funny to a lot of people*. Bunions were obviously funny to humans. I made a mental note of that for the future, then burst out laughing, until I realized that all the others had already stopped. Obviously, the laughing moment was over.

"Listen to this, everyone," the female ogre said. She held up a newspaper called *Hollywood Casting Call* and read out loud. "This afternoon's auditions. A talking lawn mower for an animated show. A blind surgeon who's very good with his hands. And a guy with a mustache for a mouthwash commercial."

"I'm going to go out for the mouthwash commercial," the male ogre said.

"Yeah, you should," the raptor agreed. "It's made for you. Your breath is so bad you could peel wallpaper."

Everyone chuckled in a very good-natured way and I couldn't help noticing how well they all got along. In so many of the Earth movies Grandma Wrinkle and I had watched, humans were always stealing from each other and having fistfights and chasing each other off cliffs in fast cars. But the people in this room seemed . . . well . . . just nice.

"Here you go, Buddy," the female ogre said, holding up the newspaper and pointing her stubby finger at me. "This audition is tailor-made for you. *Oddball Academy* is holding open auditions for a teenage male who can play an alien. Stage 42, three o'clock."

"But I've never acted before," I protested.

"That never stopped anyone in Hollywood," Luis said. "Besides, you already got the costume. Just go to the audition and read your lines. See what happens."

"I don't even know where Stage 42 is."

"I'll get you there, Buddy. No problemo."

"You would do that for me?"

"Yeah, sure. I can't wait to see your face on TV. 'Starring Buddy C. Burger, best friend of the always-talented Luis Rivera.' It's got a nice ring."

"Take it down a notch, will you?" the raptor sighed. "It's just an audition. A one in a million shot."

Everyone in the break room went on talking and eating. They had no idea that my world had just turned upside down. Not only was I on Earth, I was at Universal Studios about to audition for a part on a television show. Me, Citizen Short Nose. If I hadn't escaped my planet, by now I would have had my sensory enhancer deactivated. I would be as good as dead—a walking zombie. And now I had a chance to become everything I had ever dreamed of being—an actor, free to be creative, to express myself, and be as unique as I ever wanted to be.

While Luis ate lunch, my sensory enhancer started to act up. Apparently, it noticed the aroma of the meatloaf sandwich. Before I could stop it, it took a whiff of the sandwich and let out a loud, blustery snorty-sneeze. Then it reached for the sandwich and grabbed it out of Luis's hands.

"Drop it," I said.

It let out a little whine.

"Right now."

Reluctantly, it released its grip and I took the sandwich away and handed it back to Luis with a sheepish grin.

"Sorry," I said. "Sometimes my costume misfires."

"You should take that attachment off before your audition," Luis said. "You don't want it misfiring and attacking the producers."

While Luis finished his lunch, I paced back and forth, trying to prepare myself mentally for the audition. On my planet, each child has to appear every year before a panel of community leaders to pledge allegiance to the Squadron and recite the Regulations of the State. That was the closest I had ever come to an audition. On that day, I always felt so nervous that I actually got nauseous. My stomach was feeling the same way now.

After lunch, Luis put his Frankenstein head back on.

"I'll drop you at the stage door," he said. "After that, you're on your own."

"I won't know what to do without you. Can't you stay with me?"

"Not possible. I just took my lunch break. If I get fired, I'm back to washing dishes at my grandmother's restaurant."

"Please. It's my first audition ever."

"Come on, Luis. Stay with the kid," the male ogre urged. "I'd go with him, but I can't be late for my bad breath audition."

"Okay," Luis sighed, then turning to the tigress he said, "Olivia, can you ask Hilda the vampire to fill in for me and cover my territory?"

"Sure," she said, standing up and putting on her tiger head. "Break a leg, Buddy."

"Break a leg," all the others chimed in.

"Does having a broken leg help you get the part?" I asked Luis as we left the lunchroom.

"It means good luck, Buddy. In actor talk."

"Oh, then I hope I break both legs."

We walked down the path that led us from the lunchroom across the back lot. Trams were going by and tourists were buying food and shopping at the souvenir stalls. I smiled at everyone we passed, and said, "Hey, break a leg. And while you're at it, break an arm too."

It didn't quite get the same happy reaction it did in the lunchroom. As a matter of fact, three people told me to buzz off and one woman in a straw hat said, "I'm reporting you to your supervisor."

Then suddenly, there it was in front of us—Stage 42.

I had been expecting a happy-looking place, with people singing and dancing and performing. But this Stage 42 didn't look happy at all. It was nothing but a thick concrete wall, with a sliding metal door, a red blinking light overhead, and a gruff-looking guard standing watch outside.

"What do you want?" he growled.

"We're here for the open auditions," Luis said. "My friend is trying out for the part."

The guard looked from him to me, checking me up and down. Then he sneered, a crooked kind of grin.

"Yeah, good luck with that," he answered.

"Why thank you," I said. "I plan to break a leg."

"Fat chance" was all he said. "They're looking for a cool alien. That costume looks like you pulled it out of a dumpster the day after Halloween."

He yanked the heavy metal door open. It creaked as we went inside and were met by nothing but total darkness.

5

Luis and I just stood on Stage 42, waiting for something to happen. I couldn't see a thing. Then I remembered that I was still wearing my sunglass monocles. I popped them out and slipped them into the pocket of my space suit. Even that didn't shed any light on the situation. My eyes still couldn't adjust to the blackness in that room.

"Anybody here?" Luis called out.

"We're over here on the stage," a man's voice answered. "Follow the yellow tape on the floor. And be quiet, please, we're about to do a scene."

Luis beckoned me to follow him as he tiptoed along the yellow line of tape. It was barely visible in the darkness, so I rotated two more of my eyeballs to the front, which gave me a much better view. My suction cups seemed to adhere to the yellow tape, and each time I picked up my foot, you could hear the loud *pop, pop, pop* of the suction cups lifting off the ground.

"Cut!" came the annoyed voice from the stage.

"What is it we're supposed to cut?" I whispered to Luis. "I don't have scissors."

"I said quiet on set!" the voice bellowed. "You just ruined the take."

"What's he talking about?" I whispered to Luis. "I didn't take anything. My pockets are empty except for my monocles."

"Zip it, Buddy," Luis whispered back. "You're going to get us thrown out of here."

Suddenly, a scowling man with a ponytail appeared out

of the darkness. He looked me up and down and said, "Let me guess. You're here to audition for the alien kid."

"Wow, how'd you know?" I asked.

"Don't be a wise guy," he snapped in a not-too-friendly way.

"That's Duane Mitchell, the director," Luis whispered to me. "He's pretty famous on this lot."

"He seems to be in a bad mood," I whispered back.

"Don't kid yourself," Luis said. "That's him in a good mood."

"Enough of the whispering," the director grumbled. "I can't create in this environment. Your hushed tones are like sandpaper on my eardrums."

"I'm so sorry, Supreme Leader," I answered. "I won't even breathe through my mouth. I'll only use my nose, although that might make it hard to fill my three lungs."

"Give me a break, kid. You don't have to be an alien until you get up on the stage. Now please sit down and wait your turn. And try to keep your weird toes quiet."

Moving quickly on my tiptoes, I followed Luis around a corner where I saw some bright lights, a couple cameras on wheels, and a schoolroom with tables and comfortable chairs and couches. That looked very inviting, so I hurried over and took a seat on one of the chairs next to a teenage girl who also had a ponytail, but hers was black. She looked surprised to see me.

"Hello," I said. "I'm Buddy C. Burger."

"I don't care if you're Raymond M. Hot Dog," the director shouted. "Get off that chair. You've plopped yourself right in the middle of the set. Now go sit on those metal chairs, like the other actors who are waiting to audition."

"Don't worry about him," the girl on the couch whispered to me. "He always yells. He's in charge."

"I know someone like that," I whispered back. "The Supreme Leader of the Squadron on my planet."

"You're really in character," she giggled. Something about her laugh made me giggle too.

"Hey, kid, what is wrong with you?" The director stomped over to me and stood there with his hands on his hips. "You don't talk to the talent."

Luis stepped onto the stage and quickly grabbed me by the arm, taking me to the row of metal chairs lined up on the side of the stage.

"What'd I do wrong?" I whispered.

"That's Cassidy Cambridge," he answered. "She's the star of the show, man. You got to be respectful and keep your distance."

A woman with a clipboard came to the center of the classroom and called out a name.

"Next up is Todd Fox!"

A tall, skinny kid with blond hair stood up and slouched onto the stage. He looked like a regular human except that his face was painted green. I can't tell you how many Earth movies Grandma Wrinkle and I watched about aliens with green faces. We always wondered where humans got the silly idea that we aliens are green. And that we have six eyes. Oh wait a minute—I do have six eyes.

"Okay," the director said. "Start at the top of page four. You're the new kid in class, and you're from Mars or someplace."

"Mars?" I whispered to Luis. "What's he talking about? I passed Mars on the way here, and there was nobody on it."

Luis held his finger to his lips to shush me up.

"Cassidy, you've got the first line," the director said. "And . . . ACTION!"

The girl with the ponytail stood up from her desk and walked over to Todd. She put her hand out to shake his.

"Welcome to Oddball Academy," she said. "Looks like you'll fit right in."

"I come in peace," Todd Green Face said. He paused

for a long time, then looked down at his script and started to shuffle the pages. "Uh-oh, I lost my place," he told the director.

"I got your place," the director said. "It's outside, on the tram back to nowheresville. We have no time for this. Next!"

"Just give me one more chance," Todd whimpered.

"Preparation!" the director said. "It's an actor's best tool. You, my friend, are missing the entire tool belt. And on your way out, give your script to eyeballs over there. No use wasting good paper on a script that you haven't bothered to learn. At least we can save some trees."

As Todd walked by me, he stuck his hand out and almost threw the script at me.

"This part isn't worthy of my talent, anyway," he snarled. "You can have it."

I took the script and held it up to my forehead, letting my brain skim it quickly. It only took me a few seconds to memorize it. Before I knew it, I was on the stage, acting out the scene with Cassidy. I had never acted before, but she made me forget that. We jumped right into the scene and it felt like I was talking to an old friend.

INT. ODDBALL ACADEMY CLASSROOM — DAY

The alien is brought into the classroom
by PRINCIPAL BROADBOTTOM.

> PRINCIPAL BROADBOTTOM
> Listen up, students. This is your
> new classmate who hails from Mars.
> Let's give him a rousing Oddball
> Academy welcome.

Principal Broadbottom exits, and Cassidy
gets up from her chair. She walks to the
alien and extends her hand.

> CASSIDY
> Looks like you're going to fit
> right in here at Oddball Academy.
> You're certainly odd enough.

> ALIEN
> I come in peace.

The alien reaches out and touches
Cassidy's forehead with his finger. She
jumps, as if she's just been shocked.

                    CASSIDY
          That's one powerful finger. So,
          like, you're an actual alien.

                    ALIEN
          Yes, I bring you greetings from my
          people.

                    CASSIDY
          That's what you guys always say.
          Then you invade the world and take
          over our minds.

                    ALIEN
          Oh, I'm not that kind of an alien.
          I'm more of your nerd-type alien. I
          like to read books.

The alien walks to the teacher's desk,
picks up a book, balances it on his

head, closes his eyes for a split
second, then bursts out laughing.

                    ALIEN
          Have you read this? It's hilarious.

                    CASSIDY
          You read through the top of your
          head?

                    ALIEN
          Doesn't everyone?

                    CASSIDY
          We're all a little odd here. Take
          me. I see things. From the past.
          From the future. I communicate with
          spirits. It's my gift.

                    ALIEN
          Can you show me?

                    CASSIDY
          Sure. Who would you like to meet?

ALIEN

    I've always wanted to meet a rock
    and roll star.

Cassidy goes into a trance. In the back-
ground, music starts to play, a rhythmic
guitar riff.

Suddenly, right in the middle of the scene, my sensory enhancer shot up from my back and started to move to the beat of the music. It bounced up and down with way more enthusiasm than I would have liked because it kept knocking me off balance.

"Cut!" yelled the director. "Kill the music!"

When the music stopped, my sensory enhancer immediately settled down onto my back. Duane came stomping out from behind the cameras.

"What was that thing you did just now?" he asked.

"Oh, you mean this," I said, pointing to my sensory enhancer. "I'm so sorry. It will never happen again."

"No, I loved it. Can you do that whenever you want?"

"Most of the time."

"So you rigged up that costume with batteries? Is that it?"

I didn't know what to say. Should I reveal the truth and tell him the sensory enhancer was part of my body? That I was a real alien who had just flown billions of miles across time and space to get here? That might freak him out. I made an instant decision.

"Yeah, batteries," I said. "How'd you know?"

"Wow," the director answered. "You really take this character seriously. I'm impressed. And you learned your lines in record time. Cassidy, what do you say?"

"It was fun doing the scene with him," she said. "We had chemistry."

"Chemistry works for me," the director said. He put his hand on my shoulder.

"You're hired, kid. I'm Duane Mitchell and I'll be your director. What's your name?"

"Buddy C. Burger."

"First off, Buddy C. Burger, my advice is to drop the C. I think I can make you a star. How does that sound?"

"Unbelievable," I stammered. "I mean, truly unbelievable. Have I said the word 'unbelievable'? It actually is—un-be-liev-able."

I looked over at Luis.

Enough with the unbelievable, he mouthed.

"So, Buddy, is that a yes or a no?" Duane asked.

"That's yes with a capital YES. I say *igen!*"

Duane's face went blank. "Why would you say that?"

"That means yes in Hungarian. I need to practice my Hungarian every chance I get."

Duane shook his head. "You know, Buddy, I think you might actually be an alien."

Uh-oh. Had I been found out? But then I saw he was laughing. I laughed too, and made a mental note that I should never speak Hungarian again.

"Rehearsals start tomorrow at nine o'clock sharp here on this stage," Duane said. "Be here on time or don't be here at all. Study your lines because we tape in front of a live audience tomorrow afternoon."

"I'm so glad they're not dead," I said.

"Who's not dead?" Duane asked.

"The audience. You said we tape in front of a live audience. That's good because a dead audience would be very quiet."

"I'm just going to ignore that you said that." Duane shook his head again. "Now, I know you have a lot to learn before tomorrow, but I believe you can pull it off."

I couldn't believe what I was hearing. I had just gotten a job. As an actor. On Earth. On television.

"That's a wrap," the director called to the other actors waiting their turn. "Thanks for coming, everybody, but we've found our guy."

He grabbed his jacket and gathered up his script. As he was leaving, he turned back to me.

"By the way, you should leave your costume with the wardrobe department so they can get it dry-cleaned."

"Oh, thanks, but dry-cleaning isn't necessary," I said. "And neither is wet-cleaning. I don't sweat."

"Have it your way," he said with a shrug. "Meet me in my office in ten minutes to sign the contract. And bring your parents. You're underage, so they have to sign the contract for you."

I froze right there in my tracks.

Bring my parents?

Now, that was going to be a problem.

6

I *was in a daze as we left Stage 42 and walked back* into the sunlight.

"Dude," Luis was saying. "I've never seen anything like that in my life. New actors usually spend years waiting tables before they get their first job."

"What are they waiting for the tables to do?" I asked.

Luis laughed and slapped me on the back, which made my sensory enhancer let out a little cough. I quickly put my hand over my mouth and pretended that's where the cough was coming from.

"Be serious, Buddy," he said. "The job you just got is practically a costarring role."

"Luis, I have a big problem with this job," I said, "and I don't know what to do."

"Okay, let's sit down and talk. That's what friends are for. And now that you're a star, I'm appointing myself your best friend."

Luis headed over to a truck parked by Stage 42 and I followed him, my suction cups popping on the ground until I remembered to walk on my tiptoes. Inside the truck, I could see racks of costumes—everything from a queen's velvet robe with a jeweled collar to a space suit that looked remarkably like the uniforms of the Squadron on my planet. Luis perched himself on the open tailgate and gestured for me to sit down.

"Talk to me," he said.

I took a seat next to him.

"I can't sign the contract," I said. "I don't have parents."

"What do you mean you don't have parents? What were you, hatched from an egg?"

"Actually, it was more like a gestational pod."

Luis was my best friend—he just said so. It didn't seem right to hide the truth from him. If I was going to trust anyone with my secret, now was the time.

"Luis," I began. "I know this is hard to believe, but I actually am an alien. I come from a red dwarf planet eight galaxies away."

Luis put his head in his hands and covered his face. I thought I had made him cry. I understood. If I had met the first human to ever come to my planet, I would have cried too.

It turns out he wasn't crying. He was overwhelmed with frustration.

"Buddy, I'm going to talk to you man-to-man," he said, uncovering his face. "You are about to screw up the opportunity of a lifetime. If you continue to spout this alien nonsense, they will take the part away from you. And while we're at it, your sense of humor is wearing me out. You've got to knock it off."

I sat there on the truck and let his words sink in. These humans, even someone as nice as Luis, were not prepared to accept me for what I was. An alien was too alien for them. That hard fact left me with no choice.

"Okay," I said to Luis. "I'll knock it off. I just don't want to hurt it."

"Buddy, you're hurting my brain. Enough already."

"Okay, here's the truth," I said. "My parents are archaeologists searching for a lost city under the Sahara Desert. They're unreachable."

If you're wondering where that little gem came from, it was the plot of one of the movies Grandma Wrinkle and I loved to watch. My favorite part was when the hero fell into the pit of deadly snakes because we don't have any snakes on my planet and it was the first time I had ever seen one. But I left the snake part out.

"Archaeologists?" said Luis. "Wow, that's cool. So who's watching you?"

Another one of my favorite old movies popped into my head.

"I've run away from a boarding school for orphan boys where they feed us lumpy porridge and day-old bread. The kid in the bed next to me was named Oliver. He's the only one who knows I'm gone."

Luis didn't seem to know that movie because he believed every word I said.

"Oh man," he said. "That makes it even more important that you get this part. We can't have you sent back to the orphanage."

We sat there on the truck, thinking. A large man with a mustache was walking past us, pushing two gigantic lights on stands with wheels. Behind him two other people were taking a piece of scenery that looked like a castle drawbridge off a truck and carrying it through a stage door. A wardrobe woman in the truck we were sitting on was fitting an actress for her all-black witch's costume.

It was great here on the back lot. I wanted to stay.

"There has to be someone else who can sign for me, other than my parents," I said.

"You're a minor," Luis explained. "The only people who can sign for you are your parents or a guardian over eighteen years old."

A light went on in both our heads at the same time.

"Are you?" I asked.

"I turned eighteen the third of last month."

"Will you?" I asked.

"I'll give it a try. Of course, they may ask for proof that I'm your guardian. But hey, it's worth a try."

We found the director's office in a trailer not far from Stage 42. I would have thought a director's office would be fancier and bigger, but this was a little cubicle on wheels, next to a lot of other cubicles that said things like PROPS, TRANSPORTATION, LIGHTING, SCRIPT DEPARTMENT. Luis and I walked up the metal steps and found Duane sitting at a beat-up desk.

"Where are your parents?" he asked as soon as he saw me.

"They're treasure hunters in the Gobi Desert," Luis piped up.

"Right, and I'm King Kong," Duane snapped.

"Actually, they're archaeologists in the Sahara Desert," I explained.

"Sahara, Gobi, Mojave," Luis said, jumping in to cover for himself. "What does it matter? They're all full of sand."

"Who's going to sign for you?" Duane asked. "I can't have you working tomorrow without a signed contract."

"I'm his guardian until his parents get back," Luis said. "I'll sign."

Duane studied Luis for a moment. "And who are you, exactly?"

"Luis Rivera. I'm taking care of Buddy at the moment."

"You got proof that you're the kid's guardian?"

"Sure, but it's in my sock drawer at home. I didn't

know I was going to need it today. By the way, I'm also an actor and I'd be happy to drop off my picture and résumé anytime."

"Save the pitch," Duane said. "Today is the day we need the papers signed, so bring me what you got tomorrow, and for now, just put your name on the dotted line."

While Luis was signing the contract, Duane looked over at me.

"You'll need to get a photo identification card before you can start work. One of the production assistants will take you in the morning and show you where to get your picture taken."

"I can take him," Luis said. "After all, I am his guardian."

"Great," I said. "This costume photographs really well."

"Buddy, don't be so dense," Duane said. "It's a studio rule that everyone on the lot needs an identification photo for security purposes. That means a photo of your face, not of your costume."

"He knows that," Luis said. "He was just kidding."

"I was?"

"Yes, you *was*," Luis snapped, then turning to Duane he added, "This kid is a joke a minute."

"Maybe you can get that under control, Buddy," Duane said. "And remember, having Luis sign this contract is only temporary. As soon as your parents get back, I'll need them to officially sign it. If you're still on the show, that is."

"Of course they'll sign," I reassured him.

"Okay, then we're done here," Duane said. "I've got to get my camera shots lined up for the show. Buddy, see you tomorrow with your photo ID and your lines memorized."

Luis hurried down the metal steps and I tried to follow, but my suction cups had locked into place on the top step.

"Move it, Buddy," Luis whispered. "You got the job. Let's go before he changes his mind."

"I'm trying. Everything about me is saying yes, but my suction cups are saying no."

Luis grabbed me under my arms and yanked me up in the air. He pulled so hard I thought I left some suction cups behind, but fortunately, my species has evolved so well that they all came with me. When we were clear of the trailer, Luis turned to me and held up his hand for a high five.

"We did it," he said.

"I can't believe you did all this for me. What are we going to do now?"

"Now I'm going back to work so I don't get fired. And then I got a dinner date with Olivia. You met her in the lunchroom."

"I did?"

"Yeah, Olivia. The tiger woman. We're going out for dinner. She likes to rip apart raw meat with her teeth."

"She does?"

"It's a J-O-K-E, Buddy boy. Breaking news . . . She's not really a tiger. What about you? Can I give you a ride home? Where are you staying?"

"Oh, I don't need a ride. My place is very close."

"Okay then, Buddy. I'll meet you tomorrow morning to get you set up with your photo and then walk you over to Stage 42. Where should I pick you up?"

"How about the spaceship?" I suggested. "We both know where it is."

"Okay. Eight thirty. See you then. Don't do anything I wouldn't do."

"What exactly wouldn't you do," I asked, "so I know not to do it?"

"Anyone ever tell you that you ask too many questions?"

"My grandmother always says that there's no such thing as a dumb question."

"Well, you can tell your grandmother you just invented one. See you tomorrow morning, dude."

With a wave, Luis jogged off to the path that led back to the tourist area.

It took me a long time to find my way back to the

spaceship. By the time I got there, the sun was going down and most of the tourists had left. As I climbed into the vehicle, a guard tapped me on the shoulder. I was so startled that I must have jumped ten feet in the air.

"Can I see your identification badge?" he asked.

"Oh, I just started today. I'm getting my picture taken first thing in the morning."

I held my breath, hoping he'd believe me. There was silence, then I heard a growling noise like there was a small animal inside his stomach.

"You're lucky I'm hungry," he said, patting his belly. "I got a baloney and cheese sandwich waiting for me in the guard shed. I like it with just a touch of mustard."

"I hear mustard is great on pretzels," I said.

He nodded and I could see that we had made a mustard connection.

"I'm going to let you off with a warning," he said. "Just be sure you have your photo ID next time I see you. Now get on home."

"Sure thing," I said. "I just have to crawl in here and get my stuff."

"I get it." He grinned. "Forget your ray gun?"

"Actually, it's my laser sword," I said, laughing.

"Kids today," he said, laughing hard as he walked away.

I glanced around to make sure there was no one else in sight, crawled inside, and locked the hatch behind me.

There I was, all alone. I sat down in the pilot's seat and let the events of the day sink in. I had a new planet. I had a new best friend. And if I could somehow manage to get that identification photo, I'd have a new job. All I needed was a new face.

7

Grandma Wrinkle and I had planned a new identity for me, knowing that when I got to Earth, I was going to have to look human. She had been working on a process called biological alteration, which would use electricity to make my molecular structure shift into a human type. She had tried it first on plants, and after many failures, finally succeeded in turning honeywort into butterflies. Then she experimented with insects and was able to make an ordinary beetle look like a fire-bellied toad. It stayed that way for eight days, until its molecules reverted back to beetle form.

Her plan was to create a biological alteration device I could take with me to Earth, which would allow me to assume a human form when I needed it. While she worked on perfecting one, I worked on choosing a human face that she could program into the device. This isn't as easy as it sounds. What face would you pick, if you could look like anyone in the world?

"You should pick whoever you want," Grandma Wrinkle said. "I can't promise, but I'll try to come as close as I can."

"I don't know where to begin," I told her.

"Where you always do," she said, her six eyes gazing warmly into all six of mine. "At the movies."

I went over all the movie characters I loved. At first, I thought I wanted to look just like that hotshot fighter pilot whose face never showed fear, even when he was executing high-altitude loops and barrel rolls. But I also wanted to have the rugged look of the FBI special agent who single-handedly brought the evil mob boss to justice. Oh, but there was also the steely face of the race car driver who could handle the straightaways and the curves at top speed without even blinking.

"Those are interesting choices," Grandma Wrinkle said, "but you need to pick someone close to your age. I don't think people on Earth are used to seeing an adult face on a kid's body."

When she said that, I knew exactly who I'd want to look like. Zane Tracy. I don't know if you've heard of him, because he made movies a long time ago, but he was the star of a bunch of classics called *Zane Tracy, Teenage Zombie*

Fighter. He took on armies of zombies, and he didn't care if they wanted to eat his brains. I could watch those movies over and over and never get bored, even though I knew how they ended.

Zane Tracy. That was my guy.

I settled into the pilot seat of my spaceship and looked out the window at the empty back lot. The last time I looked out that window, it was filled with thousands of people. Now it was filled with only shadows and moonlight. Looking up at the night sky, it struck me that I was on Earth, and out there, among all those stars, was my home, which I might never see again.

I shook myself back into the present and pushed the silver button on the dashboard, which popped open a mini-projector.

"Begin now," I said.

Suddenly, Grandma Wrinkle appeared before me.

"If you are watching this, then I know your journey is complete and you have arrived safely," she said.

"I can't believe it's you, Grandma Wrinkle. It's as if you're right here with me."

I wanted to throw my arms around her and never let her go, but of course I couldn't because she was just a hologram. My sensory enhancer didn't understand that, and

when it heard her voice, it reached out in her direction, making kissing sounds. But it was only kissing air.

"You are now about to watch the instructional manual I created to help you transform into Zane Tracy," the hologram said. "The first step is to reach into the compartment that holds the titanium vial of liquid crystal."

I popped open another compartment on the dashboard. It was the wrong one. There was no titanium vial inside, but there was a nutritional wafer staring me in the face. I grabbed it and was about to take a bite when the hologram spoke up.

"If I know you, you're eating right now," Grandma Wrinkle said. "Don't. This is a time to concentrate."

That's the thing about Grandma Wrinkle. She knows me so well, I can never get away with anything. I popped open another compartment, reached my hand inside, and brought out a gleaming metal vial dangling from a chain. It fit perfectly in the palm of my hand.

"This is your amulet," Grandma Wrinkle said. "As we discussed, you must wear it around your neck at all times and never let it out of your sight. It contains liquid quartz from our planet, which transmits the electrical energy you will need for biological alteration. Put it on now. I'll wait."

I slipped the chain around my neck. The amulet felt so light it was practically weightless. It was the first time I had worn it, because Grandma Wrinkle was working on it right up until my birthday. We never had a chance to actually test it out before the Squadron came to get me.

"I have programmed the face and body of Zane Tracy and placed them inside the amulet," Grandma Wrinkle explained. "If my science is correct, when you hold the amulet in the palm of your hand and focus your mind, you will complete the electrical connection that allows your molecular structure to change. Memorize this diagram."

It was a very complicated diagram, so it took me seventeen seconds to absorb it, much longer than my usual four. Grandma Wrinkle knew that, because exactly seventeen seconds later, the hologram started talking again.

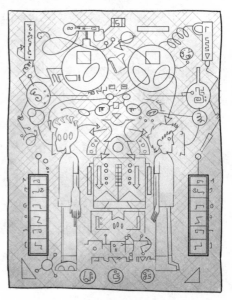

"Grandson, it's crucial that you know this. On our planet, a biological alteration lasts for three days, but remember our rotation around the sun is faster than that of Earth, and our atmosphere is different. Without having samples of Earth's air, I cannot do the calculations to figure out how long your transformation will last on Earth. You will have to find that out for yourself."

Suddenly, there was a crackling sound followed by a burst of light, and Grandma Wrinkle disappeared back into the dashboard.

"Wait," I said, pushing the silver button frantically. "Don't go! I need to know more."

My shouts were met by silence.

"Grandma Wrinkle," I called. "Can you stay with me while I try it out? I'm frightened. What if it doesn't work? What if it works too well and I can never get back to myself?"

But Grandma Wrinkle's image had disappeared. I was going to have to do this by myself. Taking a deep breath, I grasped the amulet tightly, letting all seven of my fingers wrap around my hand twice. I closed my eyes and waited for the process to begin.

I felt nothing. Opening only three of my eyes, I took a peek down at my body. There I was, my regular self, suction cups and all. What was I doing wrong?

Grandma Wrinkle had said that I had to focus. I just didn't know what to focus on. I zeroed in on the silver button on the dashboard. I was going to need all six eyes for this. I focused on it so hard that the button started to blur in front of me. But that's the only thing that happened.

I thought that maybe a memory would help me focus my energy. I visualized my best friend, Citizen Three Lips, remembering us counting star clusters in the dim light of our two moons. Back home, that was one of our favorite things to do. As I relived the memory, I could feel my life energy accelerate, and I waited for the Zane Tracy transformation to take place. Nothing happened. The only thing I felt was sadness that I might never see Citizen Three Lips again.

This was not working. I opened my eyes and, in frustration, tore the amulet off the chain and tossed it across the cabin. It landed on the pile of papers that Luis and I had just signed—my contract, a passport into my new life. A life that wasn't going to happen unless I figured this out.

8

The harsh yellow sun streaming through my spaceship
windshield woke me up with a start. Dawn on my
planet comes in pink and soft, and waking up is a slow, gentle
process. I hadn't expected my first morning on Earth to begin
with such a jolt.

I must have fallen asleep sometime in the middle of the
night, my energy zapped from the effort of attempted biological alteration. The process of becoming Zane Tracy had
never fully worked. Once or twice, I noticed that I only had
five fingers on each hand, and they were shorter and notice-
ably human. But the transformation never made it all the way
down to my suction cups or all the way up to my face. Finally, I
must have fallen asleep from the sheer exhaustion of trying to
focus my mind. My best hope was that sleep had revived my
energy and this morning's effort would result in a complete
transformation so that I'd be ready for my photo ID picture.

I reached for the chain around my neck and held the titanium amulet in the palm of my hand. Closing my eyes, I focused all of my energy on the words I repeated silently to myself.

"I am Zane. Be Zane now."

I heard the rumble of an engine outside my window. Looking out, I saw a truck drive by with two round brushes sweeping the pavement and sucking in any litter left behind on the ground. I had to work extra hard not to allow the noise to break my concentration.

"I am Zane. Be Zane now."

I reached deep inside and went to a quiet place in my mind, blocking everything else out. I visualized myself turning into a human. I saw human hair, human arms and legs, and blinking blue eyes. With every cell in my body, I concentrated on being an earthling. Nothing else existed for me.

Suddenly, I felt a swirl of electrical current under my skin, mild at first, and then growing stronger until I felt something sprout from the top of my head. I reached up with my free hand and couldn't believe what I was touching. Human hair. It was so soft and thick. My sensory enhancer, having no idea what was happening, reached up and touched it too. It must have really liked what it felt because it buried itself in my newly grown hair, playing with it like it was a furry puppy.

"That's enough," I said, pulling it away from my hair. "You're disturbing my concentration."

I closed my eyes and tried to regain my focus.

"I am Zane. Be Zane now."

My mind locked in on those words, repeating them over and over. Then the electricity in my body started to buzz and I felt a tightness all over, as if I were being encased by a flexible membrane. That could only be one thing. Human skin. I felt it creeping down my entire body, surrounding my sensory enhancer and pressing it flat against my back.

In movies, I had seen people being transformed into zombies or vampires or aliens, but now I was being transformed into a human being. And it was real. I was thrilled and terrified at the same time.

I moved my new fingers and they worked pretty well. As I watched my suction cups being covered with skin, I could feel them deflate and heard each one make a popping sound as if it were exhaling. Within seconds, the suction cups on my feet disappeared and were replaced by human toes. No offense to any of you humans out there, but those crooked little toes with sharp nails on the ends are not going to win any prizes for beauty. I wiggled my ugly new toes. They seemed to work, at least.

"Buddy! You in there?" Luis said, rapping on the hatch door. "I've been waiting here for ten minutes."

"Just give me one second," I called.

"Okay, but you better shake a leg. You've been in there so long they're going to start charging you rent."

I reached for the door handle to climb out, but stopped suddenly when I realized that I was stark naked. I was pretty sure I shouldn't go outside totally undressed. On my planet, if you are found naked outside your home space, the Squadron picks you up and throws you into a behavior readjustment program. I didn't know how humans on Earth felt about being naked in public, but I didn't want to take a chance.

I opened the compartment labeled EARTH COSTUME and pulled out a pair of jeans, a white tee shirt, and sneakers that Grandma Wrinkle had made for me. She modeled my costume on exactly what Zane Tracy wore in his movies, except in the movies, his tee shirt was covered with green zombie vomit. I stepped into the jeans, pulled the tee shirt over my newly hairy head, and laced up my red sneakers.

When I opened the door, Luis looked astonished.

"Who are you? I thought Buddy was in there."

"Luis, it's me. Buddy. In the flesh."

"Whoa . . . So that's the real you? Dude, you should never wear a costume again. You look like a movie star."

"That was the plan," I said.

"Come on, let's get going. You got a career to kick-start."

Luis turned toward the path that led from the back lot to the soundstages. I climbed down the spaceship ladder to follow him, but as soon as my feet touched the ground, I toppled over and fell right on my face. I was going to have to learn to walk on these human feet. They had a lot of moving parts and no suction to hold me in place.

Luis turned around and looked surprised to see me on the ground.

"What are you doing down there?"

"I was having trouble walking."

"Dude, put one foot in front of the other. It's not that hard."

"Easy for you to say."

Luis extended his hand and pulled me to my feet. It took a minute to get my balance, and then I tried putting one foot in front of the other. By the time we got to the security office, I had really gotten the hang of it.

The photographer had about ten earrings in one ear, and even one in her nose. That must have hurt.

"Hi," she said. "Come in. Stand right over there on the *X*." She held the camera to her face. "And no smiling."

"I wasn't going to."

"And no talking either."

Without another word, she snapped my picture. The flash from the camera blinded me just like the sun. It was so bright, it penetrated my exterior Zane Tracy eyes and made my actual six eyes underneath blink all at once.

Luis and I waited while she printed the picture and laminated it onto an identification card. She attached the card to a lanyard and put it around my neck.

"Wear this at all times when you're on the lot," she said. When she noticed the amulet that was also hanging around my neck, she let out an admiring whistle.

"I'm a jewelry geek, but I've never seen anything like that," she said. "Where'd you get it?"

"You go to the Milky Way and turn left," I said.

"Oh, the Milky Way—is that the jewelry store on Hollywood Boulevard? It's around the corner from that?"

"It depends how you define corner," I said.

Luis and I hurried across the lot and arrived at the door of Stage 42 at exactly nine o'clock.

"Okay," he said. "You're on your own."

"You're going? Just like that?"

"I'm not a star like you, dude. I have a job. That Franken-stein suit is calling. I'll come back for the taping later."

And then he was gone. I pulled open the heavy stage door and walked in, following the yellow tape like I had the day before. In front of me were two long tables that formed an L. They were piled high with all kinds of Earth food. A lot of people were clustered around, filling paper plates with cheese and fruit and cereal and yogurt and lots of round cake-like things with holes in their middles.

"Hey, new kid," a big, soft-looking woman standing behind the table called out. "Welcome to Mary's Kitchen. I see you're looking hard at those doughnuts. Can I get you one?"

"That'd be nice," I said to Mary. "But I'd like one without a hole. I'm really hungry."

Mary let out a robust laugh. "You and me, honey, we're going to get along just fine."

I was eager to try out my new mouth and see what it felt like with food inside. I took a bite of the doughnut and, wow, the flavor exploded on my tongue. It was a good thing my sensory enhancer was safely tucked away under my human skin, because if it had gotten a whiff of this doughnut thing, it would have shot into space and circled the globe three times.

"Five-minute warning," a man called out. "Cast members, gather at the table to read the script changes from last night."

Cast member . . . That was me! I stuffed the rest of the doughnut in my mouth and chewed as fast as I could. I saw Cassidy walk over to a square table near the set and sit down in a canvas chair that had her name on the back. Next to her was an empty chair, so I walked up and sat down in it.

"Hi," I said. "It's me."

"Hello me, but I don't know you."

"Yes you do. I'm Buddy Burger. Remember, I auditioned with you yesterday."

"You're the guy in the cool alien suit? In case nobody's told you, your human face is pretty cool too."

"Yeah, well that human face is sitting in my chair," a voice from behind me said.

The voice speaking was not friendly at all. It was so cold it practically had icicles dripping off it. I turned around to see who was speaking. Standing nearby was a tall boy a little older than me, with slicked-back hair and teeth so white they could glow in the dark. He was wearing large earphones around his neck. I wondered if he had ears on his neck.

"Tyler," Cassidy said to him. "There are ten chairs here. Just pick any one."

"This one has my name on it," Tyler said. "See, 'Tyler Stone.' That's my chair, and don't you forget it."

"Oh, I won't forget," I said. "I have an excellent memory."

"Who is this bozo?" Tyler asked Cassidy. *Bozo.* Hmmm . . . I didn't know that word, so my brain ran it through my Earth dictionary. The first thing that came up was that Bozo was a prince of the royal house of Serbia. I turned to Tyler and smiled.

"Thank you for the compliment," I said, "but I'm not from Serbia. And it might be hard to believe, but I'm not a prince either."

"Why don't you just take your wise-guy self out of my chair," Tyler said.

I slid out of his chair and started to sit in the one next to him, but he put his hand out to stop me.

"That one's taken too. Page Robinson, the entertainment reporter from the *Teens Today* blog, is going to sit there. She's shadowing me today for the lead story she's doing on heartthrobs. I am one, you know."

"Tyler likes to keep us updated on how wildly popular he is," Cassidy said. "He reminds us every hour on the hour."

"I can't help it if I drive my fans wild," he said. "It's a gift. You either have it or you don't." Then he slapped me on the back so hard I thought I heard my sensory enhancer whimper. "Too bad you don't have it, Buddy. And you never will."

A tall blond woman approached us, wearing heels so high that they *clickety-clack*ed on the stage floor when she walked.

"Page," Tyler said, flashing his glowing teeth. "I'm saving a chair just for you."

Page said hi to Cassidy, then looked at me and smiled.

"Are you new to the cast of *Oddball Academy*?" she asked.

"Yes, I'm playing an alien."

"Well, you don't look like an alien to me," she said. "Unless you come from the planet of handsome. Maybe I can interview you sometime."

Before I could even answer, Tyler spoke up.

"Will you excuse us for a minute, Page," he said. Then he put his arm around me like we were long-lost brothers, his hand squeezing my shoulder a little too hard, and walked me away from the table.

"Here's the deal, Buddy Burger," he snarled. "There is one male star on this show, and that's me. You're only here for a week, so just say your lines and don't bump into the furniture, and we'll get along fine. And keep your mouth shut. Is that clear?"

I wasn't sure how I was going to say my lines while keeping my mouth shut, but there was no time to think about that because the next thing I heard was "Everyone take your seats and open your scripts to page one."

It was showtime.

9

Duane Mitchell sat down at the head of the table. Along the center of the table were cups of pencils and yellow highlighters, and a script in front of each chair. Duane had a blue binder in his hands and a no-nonsense look on his face.

"All right, friends, we have no time to dawdle," he began. "We tape tonight, so let's read through the changes and get this show on its feet."

Wanting to following directions exactly, I stood up.

"What do you think you're doing?" he said to me.

"Getting myself on my feet," I said proudly.

"Are we going to have to put up with those lame jokes all day?" Tyler groaned.

"Buddy is new to the business, so maybe he doesn't know that when you put a show on its feet it means that you rehearse it walking around," Duane said.

I sat down as fast as my human butt could hit the chair. I had so much to learn.

"Everyone welcome our guest star, Buddy Burger, who's playing the new student at Oddball Academy," Duane said. "Buddy, you'll be playing an alien from the planet Zork."

"Excuse me, sir," I said, "but I know all the planets in our galaxy, and there isn't one called Zork. Even including stars and galaxies, there's Andromeda, Epsilon, Pegasi B, and, of course, PSR 1257. But no Zork."

"Duane, could you tell him to put a sock in it," Tyler said, shooting a withering look at me.

I couldn't believe I had made a second mistake so quickly. I had only been in show business for thirty seconds, and I was starting to worry they might be my last.

"I think it's fantastic that Buddy knows all that stuff," Cassidy said. "You're just jealous, Tyler."

"People, focus." Duane clapped his hands to get our attention. "We have a show to do. Buddy, here's a quick recap. *The Oddball Academy* is a comedy about a bunch of kids with unusual powers or gifts who attend a weird boarding school."

"I'm the only non-oddball," Tyler said. "I also have the most lines."

"In the show, Tyler's parents enrolled him in the Oddball Academy and left the country," Duane explained. "So

now he's stuck going to school with all these kids he has nothing in common with."

"I play Ulysses Park," an Asian kid with big blue glasses said, "which also happens to be my real name. My parents are Korean and named me Ulysses because my mom loves Greek mythology. My character is a guy whose power is that he can imitate any historical figure. Check out my George Washington: 'I'm leading the troops across the Delaware River, but, oh no, the wind just blew my wig off. Soldier, dive in and capture that wig before it gets eaten by a beaver!'"

Everyone laughed, except Tyler, who just sighed.

"Nice to meet you, Ulysses," I said.

"I play Martha Middleton," a round-faced, curly-haired girl at the table said. "In real life, my real name is actually Martha Cornfoot, but the producers didn't think Cornfoot had enough zing."

"Zing is always important," I said, choosing my words carefully so I didn't make a fool of myself a third time.

"My character is totally obsessed with musicals and she sings most of her lines," Martha said.

"Martha's voice is so big you can hear it in Nebraska," Cassidy added.

My brain processed the stored map of the United States, and quickly computed that it is 1,552.2 miles from Los

Angeles to Omaha, Nebraska. She certainly must have a big voice.

"WELCOME TO THE SHOW," Martha sang in a booming voice so loud that it made my ears vibrate even under my human skin. "WE'RE ALL GLAD YOU'RE HERE."

"And then there's me," Cassidy said. "I play a girl with extrasensory perception. My character is so clairvoyant that she can sense the future and see the past. She can even talk to dead people."

"Wow, what do they have to say?" I asked.

"What do you think they say, doof?" Tyler said. "*I'm dead.*"

That Tyler had quite an attitude. He was the only person I'd met on Earth so far who didn't want to be my friend.

Duane had us open our scripts and read our lines out loud. I wanted to be really good, so I held the script up to my forehead and let all the words seep into my brain until I knew everyone's lines by heart. That took about ten seconds. I made a note to myself that my brain seems to run a little slower on Earth. Maybe it's the gravitational pull. Grandma Wrinkle would have known. I made another note to ask her.

Oh wait. I can't ask her. I don't even know if I'll ever see her again.

There were lots of people sitting in a row behind us, taking notes as we read through the script.

"Who are all those other people?" I asked Cassidy when the reading was over.

"Everyone who works on the show," she explained. "All the department heads—you know, the people who are in charge of props and wardrobe, camera and sound. That woman over there with the red glasses is our set teacher, Janice."

"You go to school here on the show?"

"We have to put in four hours a day. But it's fun, because Janice is a great teacher. She brought in a shoebox filled with earthworms for us to study. Did you know that they breathe through their skin?"

"Lower life-forms are strange. Did you know that the colossal red sand beetle poops through its mouth?"

"Okay, you win the gross award," Cassidy said with a giggle.

A man sitting in back of us tapped her on the shoulder and pointed to the script.

"Do you like your new lines, Cassidy?" he asked.

"Yeah, they're funny. You guys did a great job."

"Who is that?" I whispered to her.

"That's one of the writers. They're the ones who look like they never go outside."

After the reading, we began the real rehearsal. Duane would tell me where to stand and help me interpret my lines. He worked with the whole cast, but mostly with me, since I was the newcomer on the show.

As the rehearsal went on, I suddenly started to feel weak and dizzy. I sat down at one of the desks in the classroom set.

"What are you doing?" Duane asked in an irritable tone of voice. "Stand up. The next break isn't for another half an hour."

I immediately jumped to my feet and tried to concentrate on his directions, but my head was spinning. Cassidy continued on with her lines and went to shake my hand, just like it said in the script. I looked down and saw that one of my Zane Tracy fingers was starting to transform back to my alien spiny finger. Quickly, I pulled my hand away from hers and put it behind my back.

"Hey," Cassidy said. "What's up with your hand? Something felt weird."

I knew right away what was happening. My earthly form was fading. I needed to recharge, and fast.

I grabbed for my amulet and held it in the palm of my hand. I shut my eyes tight and said to myself, "*I am Zane. Be Zane now.*"

Duane walked up to me, shaking his head.

"Stop fidgeting with your jewelry," he said. "It's distracting from your performance. Why don't we just take that necklace off and hold on to it for you. Wardrobe! I need you here on the double."

I clutched my amulet tighter, silently repeating, "*I am Zane. Be Zane now*" as fast as I could. Rosa, the wardrobe person, was approaching us.

"Take his necklace," Duane said to her, "and hold it for him until after the show."

"Duane, please," I begged. "It's really important that I wear this. I never take it off. It belonged to my grandmother, and it always brings me good luck. I promise I won't fidget with it."

"Okay, I'll give you one more chance. Rosa, next time he touches it, the necklace goes with you."

As they walked away, I slowly brought my hand out from behind my back. The long finger had disappeared and in its place was a regular human finger.

"You look a little pale," Cassidy said. "You're not going to barf, are you?"

I ran the word "barf" through my Earth dictionary and came up with this pleasant list: *gag, heave, hurl, regurgitate, retch, spew, upchuck, toss your cookies*. I certainly had no plans to do any of those things.

"No," I said. "I like cookies too much to toss them."

"Okay, cast," Duane called out. "Let's move on to the next scene. The writers worked on it last night and made lots of changes. The new material is on blue paper. Let's begin. Interior, Day, the school cafeteria. Ulysses, we need you on set."

Ulysses got up and joined us in the cafeteria set.

"First line is yours, Buddy," Duane called out. "I'm waiting."

I cleared my throat, looked down at the blue pages, and began to recite the script.

"Interior, Day, Cafeteria. Buddy is holding his lunch tray and notices Ulysses and Cassidy sitting at a nearby table."

"Cut!" Duane yelled. "Do you want to tell me what you're doing, Buddy?"

"Reciting the script," I said. "Just like I'm supposed to do."

"You're reading the stage directions, pal. That's the part that tells the actors what to do and where to go. You're only supposed to read your lines, which are right under your character's name."

From the nearby table, Tyler laughed really loud. "What is this, acting for kindergartners?"

He got up from his chair and threw his script down on the table.

"Let me know when you're ready for my scenes. I'll be in my dressing room, reading my fan mail. Come on, Page, you're not going to believe how many boxes of letters I get."

We rehearsed the cafeteria scene with Ulysses, who was really funny playing the art teacher, speaking as if he were the great Renaissance artist Leonardo da Vinci.

"That-a Mona Lisa," he said in a thick Italian accent. "She's a-making me nut-so. And I say to her Mona, *bellissima,* why the mysterious smile? She never answers, but I know she's thinking *That's-a for me to know and you to find out.*"

Duane got mad because Cassidy and I couldn't stop ourselves from laughing when we were supposed to be serious.

"Get all your giggles out now," he said, "because cracking yourselves up is a big no-no when we're shooting in front of a live audience."

Now that I knew what a live audience was, I felt a sudden streak of terror. Rehearsal was fun, but in just a few hours, I was going to be standing in front of a whole bunch of real human beings.

"How many people are out there?" I asked Duane.

"See those bleachers across from the set? They hold three hundred people and every seat is going to be full."

I could feel my heart start to beat faster and my third lung kick into gear like it does when I'm really scared. Under my Zane Tracy skin, I could feel my real chest heaving.

"Do you get nervous?" I whispered to Cassidy.

"Sure, everybody does," she whispered back. "That adrenaline rush before a show makes you a better actor. The time to worry is when you're not nervous."

That didn't make any sense to me, but Cassidy had been in a hundred shows, so I assumed she knew what she was talking about.

We did the scene a few more times until Duane was satisfied.

"Buddy, take a few minutes to run your lines with Kate, the script supervisor," he said. "Then go to dinner, eat light, and get your costume on for the dress rehearsal."

"My costume?" I gulped.

"Yeah, your costume from yesterday," Duane said. "The thing with the six eyes and that giant trunk on your back. That was killer. You brought it with you, right?"

"Are you kidding?" I said, my voice cracking. "I keep it very close to me at all times."

Duane walked off to go over the shots with the camera operator, leaving just Cassidy and me on the stage.

"Don't worry, Buddy," she said. "When people see you in that cool costume, they're going to bust a gut laughing. You'll be great."

"You're so nice to me, Cassidy. And you're beautiful too. I love the color of your skin."

Cassidy looked really surprised at that remark.

"Buddy, people don't just blurt out comments on other people's skin color."

"But I mean it in the most positive way," I told her.

"I'm biracial," Cassidy explained. "My dad is black, and my mom is white."

"Oh, how interesting. You have *both* a dad and a mom," I said. "That's so nice. And you all live together in one pod?"

"Well, actually, my parents are separated."

"Oh no!" I said. "Where were they attached to each other? At the hip? Did they have surgery? Getting separated sounds so painful."

Cassidy looked confused at first, then she burst out laughing.

"Buddy, your jokes are so corny. We're going to have fun together, you and me," Cassidy said. "See you later, alien friend."

As I watched her go, I checked to see that Duane was nowhere around, then took hold of the amulet around my neck. I was tired from a long day's work, and my jangled nerves were draining my strength even further. "You better come through for me," I whispered to the amulet. I know it's silly to talk to a piece of jewelry, but I'm just telling you what happened.

"Who are you talking to, doofoid?" Of course, it was Tyler, returning from gloating over his fan mail.

"I was just going over my lines," I stammered.

"Why bother? You're never going to be as good as me. How'd you get this job, anyway? Is your father the head of the studio?"

"My father isn't even from here."

"What happened? He saw your face and ran the other way?"

I couldn't understand why Tyler was being mean to me.

"Listen, Cheese Burger or whatever your name is," he went on. "After tonight, you're gone. This show is about me, so just don't you get in my way. And try not to have the audience boo you too loudly."

As Tyler walked away, I ran the word "boo" through my Earth dictionary. I didn't like what turned up. It said . . . *to show contempt . . . to jeer, to heckle, to hiss.*

Suddenly, I wanted to run as far away as I could, right out the stage door, back to my spaceship, and take off for parts unknown.

Anywhere would be better than this.

10

'll be honest with you—the thought of appearing in
front of a live audience terrified me. I told myself that
I had been given the chance of a lifetime, to be part of the
movies and television shows I had loved ever since I was in
my gestational pod. I thought of what Grandma Wrinkle
always said to me.

"Grandson, live your dreams, not your fears."

Grandma Wrinkle had sacrificed so much for me to go
to Earth, maybe even her life, so I could pursue my dream. I
couldn't let fear take this opportunity from me. I wouldn't.

I found the rest of the cast and crew at dinner, lined up
in front of a long table set up in a tent outside the stage.
Mary was standing behind the table, serving steak and lasagna and salads from a long row of metal serving dishes.

"Hey, little darling," she said when I took a plate and
approached the table. "What can I get you for dinner?"

"Duane said I should eat something light."

"Light, huh? How about a plate of feathers?"

"No thank you," I said. "They'd tickle my throat."

Mary burst out into that big laugh of hers.

Mary made a plate for me that was definitely not light. There was a green salad, a square of lasagna, which she said would give me carb energy, and a piece of smelly bread she called garlic bread. It was a strong odor. Even under my Zane Tracy skin, I could hear my sensory enhancer start to snort. I hoped Mary didn't hear it, but she did.

"I apologize," I said. "I don't usually snort in public."

"That's okay, honey," Mary said with a laugh. "A good piece of cheesy garlic bread makes me snort too."

I reached for a piece of corn on the cob, which I had seen so many times in movies. It looked like an interesting thing to eat.

"Put that back, little darling," Mary said. "That's not for you."

"But I've always wanted to try it."

"An actor never eats corn on the cob before a performance," Mary warned. "It sticks in your teeth, and trust me, no one at home wants to see your dinner hanging off those teeth."

"Oh, thanks, I'll remember that. Is there anything else I shouldn't eat?"

"Lay off the almonds and spinach. They'll make your mouth look like modern art."

Earth food was not only colorful, it was weird. The salad required a lot of chewing. The lasagna splattered all over the front of my shirt. But the garlic bread, that was a whole other thing. It tasted so delicious it made my mouth water like Niagara Falls. I kept going back for more. When I was on my fourth piece, Luis popped into the tent to say hi. He was still in his Frankenstein suit, at least from the neck down, but said that he'd be done with work by the time we did the show, and he'd come watch the taping.

"Oh, and here's some advice," he said. "Go easy on that garlic bread, dude. Trust me, not only will it give you dragon breath, it will make your stomach do jumping jacks."

After dinner, Kate the script supervisor came and took

me to my dressing room. It was in a little metal trailer outside the stage.

"You want to change into your costume while we're going
over your lines?" Kate asked. "I won't look."

"Uh, I'm a little shy about stuff like that," I said.

"Fine. Here's the latest script." She handed me some
green pages. "It's got the final rewrites. You better learn your
new lines fast. The show is in ten minutes."

I held the script up to my forehead for a few seconds.

"I'm ready," I told her.

"Do you at least want to read your new lines?"

I couldn't explain that I already had, so I took the pages
and pretended to study them. We went over the lines, and I
got everything right on the first read through.

"You're a quick study," Kate said. "Get in your costume
and I'll see you on set."

When Kate left, I took my amulet and held it tightly in
the palm of my hand. I closed my eyes and visualized the
alien me. I could feel the titanium of the amulet start to heat
up as the liquid crystal inside began to bubble.

Be the real me, I thought over and over again. I opened
one eye and glanced down at my hand. It still had five human
fingers, but they were getting longer and were looking more
like my alien hands.

"*Be the real me,*" I repeated out loud, clutching the amulet. Suddenly, there was a knock on the door.

"It's Rosa from wardrobe, Buddy," the voice called. "Here to help you with your costume."

I saw the doorknob start to turn.

"Don't come in," I called out, panic in my voice. "I'm not ready."

I dropped the amulet and shoved my hands in back of me, in case she came in. Luckily, the doorknob stopped turning.

"Okay," she called. "Come find me if you need me."

I picked up the amulet again, but it took a minute to get my concentration back. In just those few seconds, the amulet had grown cooler and my fingers had shrunk back to earthling size.

"*Be the real me, be the real me.*"

I visualized myself on my home planet, running across the red sand with my suction cups popping, my sensory enhancer waving, and my six eyes scanning the horizon. Centering all my powers of concentration on that image, I felt an electrical current rising in my body. The hand holding the amulet grew so hot that my palm burned like I was holding a lit match. My forehead started to sweat.

Biological alteration generates heat, I remember Grandma Wrinkle saying. And boy, was I hot.

I felt like I might black out, when suddenly, I was overcome by a melting feeling. I opened one eye and glanced at the full-length mirror on the back of my dressing room door. I could actually see my Zane Tracy face dissolving into thin air. I could feel the hair on my head receding back into my skull and my familiar alien skin creeping up my neck and cheeks to cover my human face. My six eyes popped out and spun around my head. My fingers grew long and bony, two more sprouting on each hand. But, the process seemed to stop halfway down my body.

"Be the real me, be the real me now," I chanted.

Within seconds, my suction cups replaced my stubby human toes, and my sensory enhancer broke free from my lower back. It was so happy to be released from its human skin that it whirled around in circles, squealing like a piglet slipping and sliding in a puddle of mud.

"Buddy, they're calling us to the set!" It was Cassidy's voice at my door.

I opened my dressing room door, and Cassidy looked really surprised.

"Whoa," she said. "Get a load of you, Mister Alien Superstar."

"Do I look okay?"

"I've never been to another planet, but I bet those space dudes look awesome, just like you."

"Now look who's giving out the compliments," I said, smiling.

"They need you on the set, kids," a voice from the intercom on the wall called out.

"We better get going," Cassidy said.

I followed her down the hall to the stage. When we reached the set, the other cast members were already there.

"Places, everyone," Jules the stage manager said. "The audience is waiting."

At the sound of the word "audience," the reality of what I was about to do hit me. My suction cups froze, sticking to the floor like glue. I used all my strength to pry my feet off the floor and tiptoed my way backstage to where I was to wait behind the cafeteria door for my entrance.

"Curtain!" Duane called when I had barely taken my place. Suddenly, two stagehands appeared and wheeled away the red velvet curtain that concealed us from the audience, to reveal the bleachers filled with 318 earthlings. I know the exact number, because when you have six eyes, you can count things with supersonic speed.

The audience burst into wild applause, and all the cast members waved, smiled, and took a bow. Everyone but me, that is. I couldn't see the expression on my face, but it felt like a combination of terror and I'm-going-to-wet-my-pants-now.

"We love you, Tyler," a whole row of girls squealed.

"I hear you, ladies," he said.

"You guys all ready to laugh?" Duane said to the audience members.

"Yes!" everyone yelled out in unison.

"All right, then," Duane said. "We've got a good show for you."

The lights on the cafeteria set came alive. Five cameras moved into place, and the camera operators put on their headsets. Bruce, the makeup person wearing a fanny pack full of brushes, came in to give each of us a final touch-up. When he got to me and brushed a little powder on my nose, I had to hold back a gigantic sneeze. The last thing I wanted was any of my purple snot spraying all over his shirt.

Duane took his place in front of a bank of five TV monitors that showed what each camera was recording. A hush fell over the soundstage, broken only by Duane's voice shouting loud and clear.

"And ... Action!"

11

THE ODDBALL ACADEMY
EPISODE #37 — ODDBALL FROM OUTER SPACE
FINAL SHOOTING SCRIPT

INT. CAFETERIA — DAY

Cassidy, Ulysses, and Tyler are sitting at a cafeteria table, their trays in front of them, surrounded by the other Oddball students. Buddy enters through the cafeteria door and stands there tentatively, trying to figure out how to get his lunch. Martha enters from the hall, strikes a pose, and bursts into song.

MARTHA

    (singing)
Hello and welcome
Come in, be near
New alien kid
So glad you're here.

TYLER

Put a sock in it, Martha. My ears
need a break.
This isn't Broadway, it's a flip-
pin' school cafeteria.

CASSIDY
(to Buddy)
Just ignore Tyler. He thinks he's
better than all of us.

TYLER
It's tough being the only normal
one in the nutball factory.

ULYSSES
Lay off, Ego Man. We're not nut-
balls, we're dreamers, like the
great Beatle John Lennon.
(switching to a John Lennon Liv-
erpool accent) "You may say I'm
a dreamer . . ."

TYLER
You're not a dreamer, you're a
nightmare.

CASSIDY
Bring your tray over here, space
guy. You're one of us now.

                    MARTHA

I was in a play once about an alien.
I played his mutant musical child.

                    TYLER

That wouldn't take a lot of
acting.

                    MARTHA

The critics said it was a career-
defining performance.

Buddy the Alien has found a tray and
carries it over to the table and sits
down with the others. He picks up his
fork and gobbles down the food on the
tray.

                    CASSIDY

So, Buddy, tell us about life on
your planet. I've never met an
extraterrestrial.

TYLER

Except Ulysses.

ULYSSES

Yup, I've spent some time on the
moon. Have you?
        (whips out a space helmet and
        breaks into Neil Armstrong)
"One small step for man, one giant
step for mankind."

TYLER

It's outbursts like that that make
me count the days until spring
break when I can take me and my abs
to the beach.
        (pause for screams from the au-
        dience)
My pecs will be there too, lookin'
sharp as usual.

CASSIDY

I see your abs taking a face-plant
off a surfboard. Oops, I see a

booger hanging from your nose too.
Watch out for that.

Cassidy, Martha, and Buddy and the rest of
the kids laugh. Cassidy turns to Buddy.

                    CASSIDY
Tell us about life on your planet.

                    BUDDY THE ALIEN
Well, on my planet we have 74
moons. All the movie theaters are

on Moon 33. Moon 11 is the mall planet where we hang out and drink tungsten smoothies. You glow for five or six minutes afterward.

                    CASSIDY
     Cool.

As the alien continues to describe life on his planet, all the kids get absorbed in his stories, nodding enthusiastically.

                    CUT TO:

12

That's the way the scene was written in the script, and that's way it was supposed to happen in front of the audience. But things didn't quite work out that way.

The taping started out perfectly. The audience was quiet in the bleachers. From the corner of my eye, I could see Luis climbing over some people to get a seat in the third row. He gave me a nod of the head, and although I couldn't wave, I did blink rapidly at him.

Duane yelled, "ACTION!" and we began. The audience gasped in surprise when I made my entrance into the cafeteria. I wasn't sure if that was a good or bad thing, but it sure felt good. Without anyone noticing, I used eyeballs three and four to snap a wide-angle picture of the audience and stored it in the photo-album section of my brain. I wanted more than anything to send it to Grandma Wrinkle. It would have made her so happy. But at least I had the picture saved for when I see her again. If I ever see her again.

Martha burst into the doorway and belted out her musical welcome, and the audience applauded. So did I. Apparently, that's not okay if you're one of the actors. There's a thing called staying in character, where you are supposed to always act like the character you're playing in the show. Applauding for Martha was a big no-no, as I found out when I looked over at Duane behind the monitors and he was giving me the cut-it-out sign, wildly waving his hand across his neck.

I tried to stay in character for the rest of the show and did a good job until Ulysses started his John Lennon impression. Grandma Wrinkle and I had watched all the Beatles concerts in her underground cave, and we loved their music.

"Wow, Ulysses, you sound just like John Lennon," I blurted out. "That was even better than in rehearsal."

"Cut! Cut! Cut!" I heard Duane yell as he shot across the set and stomped up to me. He got close to my face, whispering to me with his back to the audience.

"There's a little thing called a script," he said angrily. "Stick to it."

"I'm sorry," I said. "I don't know what came over me."

"Just make sure it doesn't come over you again."

As Duane took his place behind the monitors, Tyler threw me the most unfriendly look in the world. Imagine how your face would look if you sucked on a whole lemon, pits and all. Then multiply that times two hundred.

"Buddy, you have to concentrate," Cassidy said. "I saw you in rehearsal. You can do this."

"No he can't," Tyler said. "He's a loser."

We started the scene again. This time, I managed to be quiet.

While Tyler was doing his abs monologue, I used the time to dig into the lunch on the tray in front of me. The food actually smelled good. My sensory enhancer thought so too. I could feel it trying to sneak around my body to get a better whiff. I thought actually eating food would add reality to my performance, so I picked up the knife and fork and started to eat everything on the tray. My lips smacked as I gummed the food and the metal utensils clanked against the china plate on the tray.

I thought it was good that I was making noise, that it added an authentic lunchroom sound. Tyler didn't share my opinion, especially when I dropped my fork right over his line about his lookin'-sharp pecs. The girls in the audience had been screaming as he flaunted his muscular frame, but when my fork bounced on the floor, they all burst out laughing.

"Duane!" Tyler shouted. "I cannot work like this. You've got to do something."

"Cut!" Duane yelled, pulling off his headset and striding over to me again. The camera operators took off their headsets too and hung them on their cameras, which told me that this conversation might go on longer than the last one.

"What do you think you're doing?" Duane said to me.

"Making lunchroom sounds. I was immersing myself in the scene."

"You never make noise when another actor is talking. It's one of the cardinal rules."

"I thought it added flavor to the scene."

"Buddy, do me a favor. Don't think. Don't *ever* think. Just do."

Duane went over to calm Tyler down, and while they were talking, I took the opportunity to apologize to the audience.

"I'm so sorry," I said to the people in the bleachers, glancing over to Luis as I spoke. "I'm brand-new at this and I'm trying as hard as I can. My little alien heart says thank you for your human understanding."

The whole crowd seemed to say "Awwww" in one sweet voice.

"I would come thank you personally," I went on, "but my suction cups are stuck to the ground."

The "Awwwww" turned into applause and laughter. I looked over at Luis, and he gave me a thumbs-up. Tyler, on the other hand, was a big thumbs-down. His eyes flashed with anger.

"I know you're here to see me," he said to the audience, "and I got a lot of good stuff coming up. Just hang in there."

Everyone got back into position, and Duane yelled, "Let's see if we can get this right. Action!"

Tyler delivered his speech with a lot of confidence, and as he got up from the table to leave the cafeteria, he stood onstage an extra few seconds to make sure the audience got a good look at his handsome self. You could tell he was loving being the center of attention. I had to admit, this guy did have a star quality.

My stomach, however, disagreed. As did my sensory enhancer.

I don't know if it was the garlic bread at dinner, or the three-bean salad on my tray, but suddenly something exploded inside me. It started with a loud roar, like I had swallowed a grizzly bear standing on its hind legs. Then it turned into a rumble, like a speeding train was racing through my intestines.

Cassidy, who was sitting next to me at the table, heard the rumble and gave me a shocked look. All I could do was shrug—this was out of my control. The train was pulling out of the station, and I knew it.

But the train didn't stop. Quite the opposite.

A fireball of gas, which felt equal to the size of one of Jupiter's moons, shot out of my sensory enhancer and exploded into the air. It was so powerful, it lifted me off

my chair. It was followed by a second burst that shot out in Tyler's direction and knocked him right off his feet. I won't get too deep into the odor here, but I will tell you that everyone on that set could have used a gas mask.

The audience's response was immediate. They screamed and laughed, pointing at my sensory enhancer, which seemed quite pleased with itself. I have never heard such laughter in my life. There were hoots, giggles, seal snorts, cackles, guffaws, and high-pitched hyena sounds. People couldn't control themselves. The laughter was contagious and seemed to go on for minutes. Duane looked surprised, and I thought he would say cut, but he didn't. He was laughing too.

Tyler glared at Duane.

"Are you going to let this happen?" he demanded.

"We're doing a comedy here, and they're laughing," Duane said with a shrug.

"Fine," Tyler said, running off the set in humiliation. "I'll be in my dressing room deodorizing."

My sensory enhancer, now relieved of its gassy buildup, took a single bow and then slid back to its position along my spine.

"Stay put," I whispered to it. "You're hogging the scene."

"Okay, people," Duane called out. "Let's move on to the next scene. Everyone who has a change of costume, go do it now. No dawdling. We'll meet on the classroom set in five minutes."

A comedian who had been hired to keep the audience's energy up was handing out candy and tee shirts and telling jokes. As the cast left to go backstage, I reluctantly edged over to Duane.

"I'm sorry that I ruined the scene," I said. "But my stomach and I were having an argument, and it won."

"The audience seems to be connecting with you, Buddy. Keep it up. And by the way, next time have Mary get you some breath mints."

"Oh, it must have been that delicious garlic bread."

"Smells like you ate the whole loaf."

My ears felt like they were on fire. He had said "next time." Did that mean they were going to ask me back to do more episodes? No, that was way too much to expect. Maybe the garlic had affected my brain too.

On the other hand, maybe he did mean there would be a next time. Just the thought of that filled me with enough confidence to do the rest of the show with total energy and focus. And boy did I have fun. My sensory enhancer did too. During the scene where Cassidy channels a rock star and plays air guitar, my sensory enhancer really let loose, spinning wildly to the beat. I had to grab it and wrestle it down my back, or it would have danced all night long.

When the show ended, we ran off the stage and the audience clapped and screamed.

"What happens now?" I asked Cassidy.

"This is the best part," she said. "It's the curtain call. That's when they introduce each one of us to the audience and we come out and take a bow. You better go take your costume off so they can see what you really look like."

"This is what I really look like," I started to say, but immediately caught myself. "Okay, I'll be right back."

I hurried to my little cubicle of a dressing room and grabbed the amulet from around my neck.

"*Be Zane now,*" I chanted to myself. "*Be Zane now. And hurry up about it.*"

I must have been still really focused from the show, because my transformation into Zane happened almost instantly. I felt the electrical buzz under my skin, then became aware of thick hair sprouting from my head. I enjoyed the feeling of the human skin encircling my body. My sensory enhancer was tired from its wild dancing. I thought I heard it let out a little snore.

"Buddy, hurry up," Cassidy called from outside my door. "Everybody's waiting."

I pulled on my clothes and flung open the door.

"Do I look okay?" I asked Cassidy, giving a quick check to make sure the transformation had gone all the way down to my feet.

"You look great," she answered. "I mean, really great."

She took my hand and led me back to the stage. We found our place in the cast line and waited for our names to be called. Duane was standing in front of the audience, holding a microphone.

"Let's hear it for Tyler Stone," Duane said. "Tyler, come out and take bow."

Tyler sauntered out and took center stage. The girls screamed and chanted, "We love you, Tyler" over and over.

"Love you back," he said, flashing them his most flirty grin. After standing there for what seemed like forever, he finally moved to the side of the stage to make room for the rest of the cast.

"Now let's make some noise for his costar, Cassidy Cambridge," Duane said.

Cassidy ran out and curtsied, waving to everybody and blowing kisses into the audience.

I noticed a woman with bright yellow hair standing off to the side wearing a lot of gold jewelry. She clapped the loudest and yelled Cassidy's name, then put two fingers in her mouth and whistled. When Cassidy went to join Tyler, the woman shouted at her.

"Don't stand so close to him," she yelled. "He's blocking you. Own that stage, Cassidy. It's yours."

Cassidy glanced at her and mouthed, *Mom, not now.*

The audience continued to applaud when Martha and Ulysses got introduced. Martha sang her thank-you, and Ulysses raised one side of his upper lip and said, "Elvis has left the building, but I'm here to say, 'Thank you, thank you very much.'" He had an accent and sounded just like the Elvis Grandma Wrinkle and I had seen in the movies.

Then it was my turn. I wondered if the audience was going to forgive me for all of my mistakes. It would be so embarrassing if Luis were the only one applauding.

"And now let's hear it for our guest star. Playing the alien . . . Buddy Burger."

I stepped out and faced the audience. Unfortunately, I had forgotten to tie my sneakers, and when I took a step forward, I tripped over my shoelace and fell flat on my face. Apparently, earthlings find falling down funny, because the audience burst into gales of laughter. Quickly, I pulled myself up and took a bow. It took a minute for me to register what happened next. As a single unit, the entire audience shot to their feet and started screaming.

"You're totally hot!" a girl in the front row shouted.

"And funny," a guy in back of her yelled.

They clapped, whistled, and stomped their feet on the bleachers. I'm going to go out on a limb here and say they liked me. Not to brag or anything, but you could even say they loved me. I felt it right down to my alien core. It was the best moment of my life. Even when I joined the rest of the cast, the audience didn't stop clapping.

"Buddy!" they called out. "We want more Buddy!"

Duane motioned for me to come back to center stage and take another bow. As I stood there basking in the applause, I suddenly felt an arm around my shoulder. I turned to see Tyler, giving me a big grin.

"Isn't he something?" he yelled to the audience. "Show him some love."

I couldn't believe my ears. Tyler was going to be my friend after all. It just took a while to win him over.

"Thanks, Ty," I said. "This is so nice of you."

Tyler smiled at the audience, and over their cheers they couldn't hear what he whispered to me.

"Enjoy your moment in the spotlight, you alien freak," he said, "because you're never going to see this stage again."

13

I **stood alone on the dark soundstage after the audience**
left, trying to absorb what had just happened to me. It
was like a dream—only it was real. Ever since I could remember, Grandma Wrinkle and I had imagined what it would be
like to be part of something so wonderful, to live in a world
filled with creativity and imagination. And now here I was,
smack-dab in the middle of this amazing world. If only I
could have shared it with Grandma Wrinkle. I imagined seeing her six eyes rotating to the front of her head and welling
up with tears as they gazed at me. I could almost feel her long
spiny fingers rubbing my bald, bumpy head.

On the stage, the camera operators were covering their
cameras with protective tarps, the prop master was boxing
up all the loose items like dishes and lunch trays from the
cafeteria set, and the sound team was disconnecting micro-
phones from the boom arms overhead. As the crew went

about their business, almost every one of them stopped to give me a compliment.

"Nice job, kid."

"Great way to bounce back."

"You got a bright future in Hollywood."

Out of the shadows, a familiar figure walked toward me.

"Hey, dude," Luis said. "You crushed it tonight."

"I had a very rocky start."

"Doesn't matter where you start, dude. It only matters where you end up. And the audience gave you a standing ovation."

"I don't think Tyler liked that."

"Guys like him, they think about nothing but themselves . . . and their teeth, their shiny white teeth."

"Well, he certainly does smile like a star."

"You do too, Buddy. Even in that freaky alien costume with the bright red gums."

I wondered what Luis would say if I told him it wasn't a costume, that the real me had red gums and no teeth, and that freaky body was my real one. Speaking of my body, I suddenly realized that it was very, very tired, so tired that I think I actually wobbled a little bit during our conversation.

"Want me to give you a ride home?" Luis asked. "You're looking like you could make friends with a pillow."

Home. Now, there was a problem. What home?

"Buddy! There you are!" Jules the stage manager called from the stage door. "Duane's looking for you. Wants to see you in his office."

"Thanks, Jules," I said. "Is now a good time?"

"No, ten minutes ago was a good time. Hustle over there. Duane's got red-hot ants in his pants."

"Oh my, that must be so uncomfortable."

"Buddy," Luis said. "This could be good news. Get a move on."

Luis and I hurried over to Duane's office in the trailer. I thought he'd be alone sitting at his beat-up desk, but Cassidy and her intense-looking mom were there with him. Up close, Cassidy's mother looked even more weighed down with jewelry than she did on the soundstage. Gold bracelets, gold necklaces, gold earrings. I happen to know that the atomic weight of gold is 196.966, so no wonder she looked like she was in a bad mood. Carrying all that weight around would put me in a bad mood too.

"Buddy, let's get right to the point," Duane said as Luis and I jammed into the tiny office. "We've all had a long night. You have a lot to learn, but I'm prepared to make you an offer."

"To do what?"

Luis gave me a hard poke in the ribs. "Just listen for once," he whispered.

"We want to write your character into the show," Duane went on. "You'd be a regular and appear every week as the alien student at Oddball Academy. What do you say?"

"I'll do the talking for him," Cassidy's mom said, wedging her way over to me. "That's what I do."

"Excuse me, ma'am," I said, holding out my hand. "I don't think we've met. I'm Buddy Cheese Burger."

"Hold the cheese," she said. "It's empty calories."

"I don't eat it," I explained. "It's my name."

"Not if I have anything to say about it," she said. "From now on, the cheese is history. I'm Delores Cambridge. I'm

Cassidy's mother-slash-manager. I manage my daughter's career, and it would be my pleasure to represent you as well."

"Oh, that's so nice of you," I said.

"That niceness is called twenty percent," Luis whispered. "Managers take twenty percent of everything you earn."

"I'd love to be on the show," I said to Duane. "It sounds like—"

"I'll take it from here," Delores interrupted. She stepped in front of me and sat down on the edge of Duane's desk. "What my client meant to say is that we'll consider your offer if you meet our terms. We'll need certain guarantees, of course—script approval, private dressing room with a mini-fridge stocked with . . ." She turned to me and whispered, "What kind of ice cream do you like?"

"I've never had ice cream."

"Fine," she said to Duane without missing a beat. "Just to make sure, we'll need three kinds of ice cream in the freezer. Cherry vanilla, chocolate chip, and butter brickle."

Delores ripped a page from a notepad on Duane's desk and wrote down several numbers, folded the paper, and slid it to Duane.

"Those are our financial terms. Of course, there'll be a bonus if we make a movie and first-class travel if you send him on a publicity tour."

"Wow," Luis whispered. "She's tough. This is the kind of manager you want."

"I think you need to slow down here, Delores." Duane held up his hands as if to protect himself from her torrent of words. "Those are pretty steep demands, and the kid is a beginner."

"Come on, Duane," Delores snapped. "You and I both know what we saw. Buddy has magic. That audience ate him up like a chopped salad, hold the egg."

"Mom," Cassidy said. "The hard-boiled egg is the best part."

"Cassidy, we're doing business here. We can discuss your food preferences in the car. Duane, do we have a deal?"

"I'm going to have to discuss this with the network executives," Duane said.

Delores jumped off the desk and snapped her fingers at us.

"Let's go, kids," she said, heading for the door. "Duane obviously isn't prepared to make a decision, so neither are we. There are a lot of other shows out there for you, Buddy. Tomorrow I'll start making calls."

I was just about to tell Delores how much I really wanted to be on *The Oddball Academy*. The last thing I wanted was to walk away from that amazing opportunity.

"Mrs. Cambridge," I began.

She held her finger to her lips. "Whatever you're about to say, don't."

She walked to the door and motioned for all of us to follow. With a deep sigh, Duane got to his feet.

"Okay, Delores," he said. "I'll go out on a limb here. I'll hire Buddy for the rest of the season and we'll see how he does. The salary you suggested is okay, but no bonuses or first-class travel. And just to show I'm a reasonable guy, I'll throw in the butter brickle ice cream."

"What about the chocolate chip and cherry vanilla?"

"Don't push me, Delores."

"Have it your way. Come on, kids. We're out of here."

She started to head out the door again.

"Okay, okay," Duane said. "You'll find all three in the mini-fridge in his dressing room on Monday."

Delores burst into a big smile and held out her ring-heavy hand to Duane.

"You got yourself a deal," she said. Then, turning to me, she added, "Stick with me, kid. The sky's the limit. Oh, and don't overindulge in the ice cream."

"Buddy, I'll have your contracts ready Monday morning," Duane said. "You can sign them at the table read."

"I didn't know that tables read," I said. "Do they sound like wood?"

"Seriously, Buddy," Duane said with a sigh. "You need to stop with the one-liners. It's exhausting. Now go home. I could use a break from all you people."

We left Duane's office and gathered in a circle at the bottom of the stairs.

"Thank you so much, Delores," I said. "I can't believe my luck."

"I make luck happen," she said.

"You sure do," Luis said. "You want to try some on me?"

Delores looked at Luis like she was noticing him for the first time.

"And who exactly are you?"

"I'm Luis, Buddy's best friend and guardian."

Delores turned to me.

"And where exactly are your parents?"

"They're archaeologists exploring sunken caves in the Sahara Desert."

"I don't know where the Sahara Desert is, but I'm pretty sure it's not in my zip code. That being the case, I'm going to be making all your business decisions."

"What about me?" Luis said. "I'm the one who signed on as his guardian."

"Well, you just got demoted to best friend," Delores told him. "I'll take it from here. Going forward, I'm Buddy's guardian and I'll represent him in all business matters."

"It's going to be fun to work with you, Buddy," Cassidy said, taking my arm. "We're going to have such a great time hanging out together on the set and in school. We just finished our unit on earthworms, and Janice says that next we're going to do robotics. Maybe we can build a robot together."

"Oh, I love to build robots," I said. "I built my first one when I was three. It was an autonomous rover craft that explored large-particle sand dunes near my home."

"Did you grow up on the beach?" Cassidy asked.

"Sort of. Just without the water."

"Where are you living, Buddy?" Delores asked. "With Luis?"

"He isn't, but he can." Luis shot me a grin. "We live above my grandma's restaurant. Her guacamole is famous from here to Jupiter."

"Really? I'll have to look for it next time I'm there," I said.

"You slay me, Buddy," Cassidy said, joining Luis and me in a big laugh.

Delores wasn't laughing. She was all business.

"Buddy, I assume since your parents are roaming the desert somewhere, you're staying with your best friend here. I'm going to recommend you come live with us until they return."

"Thanks, but I'm okay where I am," I said.

"Apparently, 'recommend' was the wrong word," Delores said. "Let me revise that sentence. Buddy, as of tonight, you're staying with us. Period."

My brain started to whirl. I had never been in a human house before, although I had seen them in the movies. I knew they had beds instead of pods like we have on our planet. And they have all these devices like toasters and dishwashers and toilets. I didn't know how to use a single one of those.

Delores was busy listing all the reasons why I should live with them.

"You can go over your lines with Cassidy every night," she said. "And I can keep an eye on you, and make sure they're treating you right on the show."

Cassidy seemed surprised at her mother's suggestion. "If Buddy comes to live with us, where's he going to sleep?" she asked.

"We'll move Eloise into your room. She can sleep on your trundle bed."

"But, Mom, she snores. She sounds like Darth Vader when she sleeps."

"I've always wanted to meet Darth Vader," I said. "*Star Wars* is my favorite movie, although it's not entirely accurate in its portrayal of deep space."

"Eloise is not Darth Vader," Cassidy said. "She's just a seven-year-old with a sinus condition."

"Cassidy, it won't kill you to share your room with her until Buddy's parents get back," Delores said. "Buddy, I'll take it from here. Get all your things and we'll put them in the car."

"I'm wearing all my things," I said.

"You don't even have a toothbrush? If you're going to be a star, dental hygiene is key. Shiny teeth photograph well, remember that. We'll go shopping tomorrow and get you some fashion-forward clothes. I'll front you the money until you get your first paycheck."

"Cool," Cassidy said to me. "We can spend the day shopping at the mall. And get a pizza for lunch."

"Excuse me, missy," Delores said. "He'll get the pizza. You'll get the chopped salad, hold the egg. It's my responsibility as your mother-slash-manager to see that you make healthy food choices. You might not like it now, but you will thank me later on."

"You just want me to look good in my costumes," Cassidy said.

"There is that too," Delores answered. "It's a harsh fact, but true—the camera adds ten pounds to you. Trust me, pizza is not your friend."

At the sound of the word "pizza," my whole body twitched. My stomach was still recovering from dinner. Earth food and I were not having a good relationship. The one food I knew my system could digest, the remaining nutritional wafer, was in my spaceship, which was so close and yet so far away.

I was hungry and thirsty and queasy at the same time. In all the excitement of the day, I had forgotten to drink any water. What I was feeling was more than just regular thirst, though. It was as if some unknown force were sucking all the liquid from my body. Was this terrible feeling my life force starting to dim?

Luis gave me his phone number and said to call him when I was settled in. Cassidy and I climbed in the back seat of Delores's station wagon, and we drove through the main gate of the studio.

"So long, Scotty," Delores called out to the guard at the main gate.

As we left the lot and drove onto the freeway, my head began to spin. I put it between my knees to try to get rid of the dizziness.

"Do you get carsick?" Cassidy asked.

"Yeah, carsick," I murmured. "That must be it."

"That sucks," Cassidy said. "I used to get carsick too."

There was no way to explain to her that what I was feeling wasn't carsick. I felt like my insides were drying out and turning to dust. What if I suddenly blurted out, "I'm not carsick. This is just my life force dimming"?

How weird would that be?

Pretty darn weird.

14

Luckily, Cassidy's house was close to Universal Studios, up a winding road that led to a cluster of woodsy hillside homes. Her family's house had so many glass windows you could hardly tell the inside from the outside. Cassidy's dad, a tall man with a lot of hair on his face but none on his head, was waiting for us on the front porch. Standing next to him was the cutest little girl you'd ever want to see. She had two curly pigtails on her head.

"Hi, guys," the little girl shouted before the car had even come to a full stop. "Wait until you see what Daddy and I built tonight. It's a recycling center for our city."

"That's my little sister, Eloise," Cassidy whispered.

"She seems peppy."

"You mean annoying. She is totally Lego obsessed. She wants to be an architect like our dad, and for months now they've been building Eloise-ville. Keep your distance because she leaves a trail of Legos everywhere, and those things kill when you step on them."

I didn't understand one word Cassidy said, but I was feeling too dizzy and drained to run Lego through my Earth dictionary. I tried, but it shut down after "leg" and I already knew what that was. When I climbed out of the car, I was unsteady on my feet, and Cassidy's dad's powerful handshake didn't help my balance any. He nearly lifted me off the ground.

"I'm Brian Cambridge," he said. "You must be the young man Delores texted me about. She says you've got talent and she's going to mold you into a star. Watch out, kid, she's a molder of the first order. Look at me, I used to be short and hairy. Now I'm tall and bald."

"Did she do a biological alteration on you?" I asked.

Mr. Cambridge gave me a strange look.

"Daddy, you just met Buddy the comedian," Cassidy said. "He loves to joke around."

"I know a joke," Eloise said. "Why was six afraid of seven?"

"That's easy," I said. "Because six is the smallest number that is neither a prime number nor a square number. Everyone thinks that's funny."

"Eeuuww, you're weird," Eloise said. "The real answer is because seven eight nine."

Eloise laughed so hard that her eyes watered and her nose dripped.

"Mom, am I seriously going to have to share a room with this person?" Cassidy said, rolling her eyes. "Look at her, she's like a leaky faucet."

"I'll put a box of Kleenex in your room," Delores said. "Brian, can you help the girls pull out the trundle bed in Cassidy's room. I'm giving Buddy Eloise's room temporarily."

Eloise jumped up and down, clapping her hands and twirling around.

"I'm moving in with you!" she said to Cassidy.

"You're weird," Cassidy said to her. "Most little kids would hate to leave their room. I wish you did."

"I'm not sad," Eloise said. "This is going to be so much fun. We can tell ghost stories and have unicorn tea parties and play with homemade slime."

"Mom, are you hearing this?" Cassidy said. "It is totally unacceptable."

"You'll get used to it," Delores answered. "End of conversation."

I felt like if I didn't get some water and lie down soon, I was going to pass out. As we walked inside, Cassidy was busy chatting about the house, pointing out the family photographs on the wall. Her words sounded fuzzy and far away.

"Excuse me, could I get a glass of water?" I asked, interrupting her.

We went into the kitchen, where Cassidy pulled a glass out of the cabinet and filled it with tap water. I gulped it down in one swallow, and immediately asked for another one. And another one. And another one. And another.

"Boy, you were really parched," Cassidy said.

"I bet if you jump up and down, you can hear the water slosh around in your tummy," Eloise said.

As if it had heard its name being called, my stomach let out a long, slow gurgling sound.

"Eeuuww," Eloise said. "You're not going to fart, are you?

I hate it when boys fart. Like Anthony de la Rosa. Whenever he brings string cheese for lunch, he farts up a storm."

"Mom," Cassidy said. "Can you please teach her not to say 'fart' in public?"

"Okay, okay," Eloise said. Then taking my hand, she said, "Come on, Buddy. I'll show you around if you promise not to expel gas. Is that better, Cassidy?"

The five glasses of water had revived me enough so I could walk down the hall without passing out. We left Delores in the kitchen, picking up messages from her phone while putting bananas into a food blender and typing on her computer at the same time. Cassidy said her mom called that multitasking.

The first bedroom we came to was Eloise's, soon to be mine. There were rainbows painted on the walls, and fluorescent stickers of stars and planets plastered all over the ceiling.

"All those stickers glow in the dark," Eloise said. "I say good night to every planet up there. My favorite is Saturn because of the pretty rings."

"The rings are even more beautiful in real life," I said, remembering the glowing shades of brown, gray, and pink I had just seen the day before.

"How would you know?" she asked. "Have you been there?"

"Don't be ridiculous, Eloise," Cassidy said. "No one has ever been to Saturn."

These humans had a lot to learn.

"Over there is my dresser with my unicorn collection on top," Eloise continued. "Don't touch it. There's a little comb for styling their manes. Don't touch it. And over there on my nightstand is my jar of sour gummy dragons. The best ones are the purple ones, but don't touch them. Actually, I'm taking them with me. Cassidy, I'm keeping them right next to my pillow for middle-of-the-night snacks."

"Fine, go ahead and rot your teeth," Cassidy said. "See if I care."

Eloise went on with her tour. "And over there is the bathroom I share with Cassidy," she said. "She makes you knock first."

"And what's that?" I asked, pointing to a long wooden door resting on two stools that ran down the middle of her room. It was covered with colorful plastic building blocks.

"That's Eloise-ville, silly. Daddy and I are building a whole Lego city named after me. We work on it every time Cassidy has a show night."

"Maybe I can help you guys build a space station?" I volunteered.

"Hands off," she said. "See the sign on the table? DO NOT TOUCH. It's just for me and Daddy."

Mr. Cambridge came into the room and swooped Eloise up in his arms.

"I'm taking off now, jelly bean," he said. "You got a big kiss for Dad?"

"See you next week, Daddy," Eloise said. "Remember, we're building the supermarket." She gave him a slobbery kiss on the cheek.

"Nice meeting you, Buddy," he said.

"Would you like a big kiss from me too?" I asked. I wanted to fit in with the family customs.

"A handshake will do just fine," he said. He gave me another one of his power handshakes, but this time I managed to stay on my feet.

"One last piggyback ride," Eloise said. Mr. Cambridge bent down and she climbed up on his back. "Giddyup," she giggled as they headed off down the hall toward the front door.

"Your father doesn't live here?" I asked Cassidy when they were out of sight.

"Remember, I told you my parents are separated. It's a trial separation, because they have issues."

"Because she's so bossy and doesn't let anyone else talk?"

Cassidy burst out laughing. "Wow, Buddy, you certainly call it like it is."

I was suddenly overcome with a wave of weakness so strong I thought I was going to collapse right where I was standing.

"Cassidy, could you leave now?" I blurted out.

She looked surprised, hurt even.

"It's not that I want you to leave," I added quickly. "It's that I need you to."

"You are quite the mystery person," Cassidy said.

"You have no idea," I said, practically pushing her out of my room. I didn't mean to be rude, but I had to do something about my physical condition. My mouth was so dry. My human eyes burned. I could see tiny cracks forming in my Zane Tracy hands and arms.

Water. I needed water. Not just drinking water either. I needed to submerge myself in it. Soak in it. Flood myself with it. Absorb it through every pore in my alien skin. I had waited way too long to hydrate myself. Grandma Wrinkle had warned me that without proper hydration, my life force would dry up. What was going to happen to me? Would I shrivel up? Shrink to the size of a molecule and wither away?

I looked around the room desperately, and then my eyes focused on the door to the bathroom. I wobbled over to it and pushed it open. Yes. There it was. A bathtub.

Pulling off my Zane Tracy clothes, I dropped to my knees, crawled across the cold tile floor, and climbed up and over into the tub. It was so high and I was so weak, it felt like climbing a mountain. Once inside, I couldn't lift my arms to turn on the water, so I used the suction cups starting to sprout on my feet to grasp the handles. When I finally got the water on, I noticed that the tub didn't fill up. All the water was going down the hole at the bottom. I was just able to reach a silver lever sticking out of the wall, and when I pushed it down, the drain closed. Water started to fill the tub. I grabbed the titanium amulet around my neck and held it in the palm of my hand.

"*Be the real me*," I chanted. "*Be the real me now.*"

I felt that melting sensation as my human skin began to dissolve. My fourteen bony fingers poked out of my soft human hands. My hair receded into my scalp. I looked down and saw all of my suction cups replacing my toes.

As I sank into the steaming bathwater, it was my desperate, urgent hope that my mixed-up body would be able to survive here on Earth.

15

The hot bathwater penetrated my scaly skin, and I could feel myself absorbing it like a sponge. It was as if my whole body were gulping every last drop of water. Back on my planet, there is no such thing as a "bath." We have cleaning drones that travel up and down our bodies, sucking up all the red dust particles that have attached themselves to us. (Be warned, if you ever get a cleaning drone as a gift, it does tickle when it sweeps the back of your knees.) After the drone has removed all the dirt and grime, it sprays us with essence of honeywort so we smell fresh.

I closed all six of my eyes and lay motionless at the bottom of the tub. My life force was renewing itself just as Grandma Wrinkle had promised. I could feel the water molecules helping my cells bind together again, repairing the breakdown that my body had begun to experience. But the process seemed to be taking a very long time.

What if it took all weekend? I couldn't take the bathtub to the mall.

"Buddy!"

I thought I heard someone calling my name, but with so much water in my ears, I couldn't be sure.

"Buddy! Can you hear me?" This time the voice was accompanied by someone knocking on the bathroom door.

I popped my head out of the water with a splash.

"Buddy, you're not going to believe what I've just found!"

Cassidy was in Eloise's room, shouting through the locked bathroom door.

Or was it locked? Oh no. I rotated all my eyes to the door, but I couldn't tell. I jumped out of the tub and grabbed the first thing I saw hanging on the back of the door. It was a fluffy pink robe with a unicorn horn on its hood.

"Buddy!" Cassidy called. "Come out here this minute! It's *really, really* important."

"I'll be right there," I called.

Grabbing the titanium amulet in the palm of my hand, I concentrated with all my might, and whispered, "*Be Zane now. Be Zane now.*"

Oh my gosh, I was getting good at this. Within seconds, human hair sprouted like weeds from my head, and it was even wet. Looking in the steamy mirror, I watched as my alien face transformed into Zane and my bony arms and spiny fingers disappeared under my human skin.

"Buddy, your eyes are going to pop right out of your head when you see this!" Cassidy called.

Thank goodness I only had two eyes now. Six eyes popping out of my head would be messy, and I'd also have to run around picking them up from the floor like marbles. That would be hard because they could see me but I couldn't see them.

One final check in the mirror showed me that all my eyes were safe under my Zane face. I closed the unicorn robe and tied the belt around my waist, took a breath to compose myself, and pulled open the door that led to Eloise's room.

Cassidy was jumping up and down in the middle of the bedroom, holding a laptop computer.

"You've gone viral!" she said, her eyes glued to the screen.

"I don't think I have a virus," I answered. "I was feeling weak, but I'm much better now."

"No, gone viral on the internet," she said. "Someone in the audience recorded your big scene on the show. It's only been up for five minutes, but you already have thousands of hits. Look at these comments! Everyone thinks you're so funny."

She flashed me a gigantic smile. Then she noticed the pink unicorn robe and burst into laughter.

"Don't let any of your new fans see you in that," she howled.

I joined in her laughter, and I thought we were sharing a great moment, when suddenly, her expression changed and her laughter evaporated. I followed her gaze and saw that she was staring at my feet. They were still my alien legs with the suction cups attached. Apparently, my transformation to Zane Tracy hadn't gone as quickly as I'd thought.

"Why did you take a bath with your costume on?" she said.

"Now that is a very interesting question," I answered, saying the words slowly to give myself time to think. "Um . . . I left my costume feet on . . . because I walked around on them all day, and they get dirty. It's a known fact that suction cups don't adhere well when they are clogged with particulate matter."

"Particulate matter?"

"I believe you would call that dirt."

"Listen, Buddy, if you're going to be as big a star as all these internet hits are indicating, you're going to have to knock off that 'particulate matter' talk and stick with 'dirt.' You don't want to weird out your new fans."

She held up her computer screen so we could both see it and played me the clip someone had put together of the moment on the show when I farted and when I took my bow as Zane Tracy. It was the first time I'd ever seen my two selves on video. It was thrilling.

"Whether you know it or not, you're a star," Cassidy said. "This is going to be so good for our show. We used to be the number one rated show in kids' programs, but lately our ratings have been sagging. You could shoot us right back to the top slot."

My mind was racing with the excitement of Cassidy's vision, so at first I didn't notice the slight movement coming from the middle of my back. But very soon, it became impossible to miss. My sensory enhancer was coming alive and was on the hunt for something.

"Oh no," I said out loud. "This is not good news."

"Trust me," Cassidy said. "I've been in television since I was three, and this is spectacular news."

"Your news is not the same as my news," I said.

Just then, my sensory enhancer totally escaped from the pink robe. It shot past the unicorn hood, burst into the open air, and started snorting like a hungry rhinoceros. Cassidy opened her mouth to scream, but nothing came out. Her eyes got as big as the flying saucers we use as taxis on our planet.

My sensory enhancer had gone completely wild, snorting and grunting and spinning around and around so fast I thought it was going to throw up. It jerked me around the room as it searched for the source of what it was smelling. First it rummaged in the closet, picked up a gym shoe, and took a giant whiff. Letting out a disgusted squeal, it tossed the sneaker across the room. It whizzed right by Cassidy's head, but she was in such shock, she didn't even duck. Luckily, since they don't have eyes of their own, sensory enhancers are known for having bad aim.

Next it pulled me over to the dresser and knocked over a bunch of little glass bottles of perfume. Liquid spilled out of each one, forming a small puddle so stinky it made my nose itch all the way across the room.

"Ah-choo!" I sneezed.

"Ah-cheer!" Cassidy sneezed.

"HA-HA-HA-HA-CHOO-UMMMM!" my sensory enhancer sneezed.

Air came blasting out of it with such force that it blew the bedspread right off the bed. The sunflower-patterned fabric circled in the air like a flying carpet until it landed on top of my enhancer, draping around it like a floral superhero cape. Any other time, I might have laughed at the sight, but this was no time for humor.

There was no controlling this rampage. Whatever my sensory enhancer was smelling, it wanted badly . . . and immediately. Wildly, it dragged me toward the bed as I helplessly watched it pick up the pillows and toss them around. And then, sensing that it had arrived at its destination, it froze in midair, snorting vigorously. It had found what it was looking for.

Tucked under the bed pillows was Eloise's hidden stash of sour gummy dragons. My enhancer sniffed the bag and let out a yelp of delight. With great speed and precision, it snatched the plastic bag from the bed, ripped it open, and inhaled a handful of the gummy dragons.

The sour gummies disappeared into its long trunk, and it let out a contented sigh, which was followed by total silence.

The room was completely still.

But the silence only lasted a few seconds because as soon as the sour taste of the candies made contact with the sensory buds inside my enhancer, chaos broke loose. A burst of sour gummy dragons came flying out of its snout like cannonballs, propelled with such force they embedded themselves in the ceiling.

Smack! Thwack! Zwak!

One by one, each sour gummy dragon was expelled from my sensory enhancer and catapulted into the air until the ceiling was covered with them. When it had gotten rid of the last of the sour dragons, my sensory enhancer went into a frenzy of sneezing and coughing, trying to get rid of the sour taste left behind. And then it was quiet, as if recovering from the assault on its sensory receivers.

In all the frenzy, I hadn't had the courage to check on Cassidy, to see how this was affecting her. But I knew I had to face this moment. I turned to her, and not surprisingly, she looked like she had seen a ghost. Actually, she looked like she had seen a crowd of ghosts, zombies, vampires, werewolves, mummies, banshees, and any other undead creature you've ever heard of.

"I can explain," I said.

"No!" she said, her voice trembling. "Tell me I didn't see what I just saw."

I took a few steps toward her, and she took a few steps back.

"Cassidy," I began.

"Don't even talk to me," she said. "You're a freak. What I just saw attached to your back was not human."

"You're right," I said. "I'm not human. Cassidy, I'm an alien."

She gasped and ran for the door.

"Just give me a minute, and I'll explain."

She was shaking from head to toe and crying.

"I don't understand anything you're saying. I thought you were my friend." She looked me right in the eye with an intensity that made me really uncomfortable. "Who are you? Where are you from? And what is that *thing* on your back?"

"It's my sensory enhancer," I said. "Everyone on my planet is born with one, but they get deactivated when you turn thirteen. That's why I'm here."

Cassidy covered her ears with her hands and started to hum, like she was trying to block out everything I was saying.

"I feel like I'm in the plot of a bad sci-fi movie," she said. "And I hate sci-fi, so I'm out of here Buddy or Zork or Space

Man or Captain Zoom or whatever you call yourself. I'm going to tell my mom and the police and the FBI."

"Please don't call the authorities," I begged. "They will lock me up and study me. They'll poke me and prod me and I won't be able to do *Oddball Academy*, either. I'll never be free again."

"Fine," she said. "I won't call anyone. Just leave and go back to your rocket ship and fly back to your planet, because I am not a big fan of hanging out with aliens. And you can take that snorty-gulpy thing on your back with you."

"Cassidy," I said. "Please calm down and listen."

"Get out of my way," she snapped, flinging open the door. "I am going to the kitchen to get a healthy snack. Actually, forget that. I'm going to get a chocolate-dipped mint ice cream sandwich. And I don't care what my mother says, because I think I deserve anything I want right now. And when I come back, you had better be gone and never return to this house again."

She stomped out of the room without a backward glance. I watched her walk down the hall toward the kitchen, taking all my hopes and dreams for my life on Earth with her.

16

I *watched Cassidy disappear, then turned and went* back into my bedroom—actually I went back into what *had been* my bedroom until my sensory enhancer decided to blow up my life. And I mean, literally, *blow up* my life.

"I hope you're satisfied," I said to it, but its only response was a small squeak of a hiccup. It was weak from all the sugar and excitement, and frankly, so was I.

I sat down on Eloise's bed and tried to figure out what to do. Where would I go? I felt so alone. Even though thousands of fans were liking me on social media, I was still alone. Maybe I was a viral superstar, but inside I was nothing but a blob of shaky, scared jelly. An alien kid with nowhere to go.

I put my Zane Tracy head in my Zane Tracy hands and tried to think creatively. I had seen a House of Pancakes from the freeway that said it was open twenty-four hours. I could go there and just keep ordering stacks of pancakes until the sun came up. But I didn't have any money, and besides, my stomach was still in a very bad mood from all that garlic bread. Gallons of melted butter and syrup probably would not help the situation.

I could sneak back to the Universal lot and spend the night in my rocket ship. That worked once, but it wouldn't work again. That guard—the one who liked baloney sandwiches—would turn me in for sure this time.

I could call Luis and tell him it didn't work out with Cassidy. He'd ask what happened. And I'd make up a story like her family has a whole lot of cats and I'm allergic to cats. But what if Luis's family had cats too? Then what would I say?

I rubbed my head, and even in my worried state, I noticed the soft, fluffy texture of human hair. I wondered if way back in our evolution, the citizens of my planet had hair too. Maybe the hot temperatures from our red dwarf sun caused us to shed all our hair.

"You know, you look pretty stupid in that unicorn robe."

The voice from the hall totally startled me.

"Cassidy?" I said. "I thought you were going to get an ice cream sandwich."

"I did, but I was intercepted by my mother. She took it out of my hands before I could even take a bite and gave me this instead." Cassidy held up a large stalk of celery. "This is only six calories, plus you use up one calorie chewing the stupid thing."

My Earth dictionary told me that a calorie is the amount of heat required to raise the temperature of one gram of water by one degree Celsius. Why would Cassidy's mother care about that? Cassidy must have seen the confusion on my face because she added, "My mother is a professional calorie counter."

"Oh, is she a chemist as well as your manager?" I asked. "That's very impressive."

"It's more like a hobby than a profession," Cassidy said. "She counts the calories of everything that goes into my mouth."

"Why?"

"I guess there's no such thing as an overweight alien on your planet," Cassidy said. "But here on Earth, if you want to be a TV star, you have to look a certain way. At least that's what my mom believes. She watches everything I eat like a hawk. It's so depressing."

"But you should eat when you're hungry," I said. "That's why you get hungry. It's your body letting you know that you need nourishment."

"Tell that to my mom," Cassidy said.

"I'd be happy to. Where is she right about now?"

I noticed that Cassidy had taken a few steps into the bedroom. To my surprise, she flopped onto the chair next to the bed, picked up a beige furry pillow that was shaped like a puppy, and held it tightly in her lap.

"All my mom cares about is that I'm a star," she said, petting the puppy pillow. "My career is her whole life."

"What about her life?" I asked. "Doesn't she care about that?"

"She always wanted to be an actress, but things didn't work out. No matter how many acting classes she took or auditions she went to, she just never got discovered. Bad luck, I guess."

"Oh, what she needed was to break a leg or two," I said, nodding. Cassidy gave me a strange look. "That's actor talk, you know."

"Yes, I know," Cassidy said. "In case you haven't noticed, I'm an actor too."

"I'm sorry about your mother," I said. "She must be so disappointed, because so far, this acting stuff is a lot of fun."

"She promised herself that I would have the success she never got," Cassidy said. "But the bad part is I have to be perfect for her all the time. She doesn't even want to know about any part of me that isn't perfect. When I was just a baby, she had me doing modeling for baby food ads. Then she put me in one kiddy beauty pageant after another. I could never just play with the other kids. I had to be in talent contests and wear sequined dresses and tons of hair spray."

"You sprayed your hair on?" I asked. "Why, were you bald? Not that it's bad to be bald. Everyone on my planet is, including me."

That comment seemed to jolt Cassidy back to reality. She jumped up from the chair, dropped the puppy pillow, and looked at me uncomfortably.

"For a minute, I forgot that you were an alien," she said. "I was just talking to Buddy."

"You *are* talking to Buddy," I said. Then realizing that my suction cup feet were still sticking out from the unicorn robe, I added, "Just don't look below my knees."

"Who is the real you?" Cassidy asked. "The alien with those weird sucker toes and the wild trunk on his back? Or Buddy C. Burger, really nice guy?"

"I'm both," I said. "Inside, I'm an alien. Outside, I'm a human. But they're both part of the real me."

Cassidy thought about that for a long time.

"Actually, that's just like me," she said. "There's the real me on the inside, and then there's the star me on the outside."

"I like them both," I told her. "Maybe you could like both of me too?"

"To tell you the truth, those toes of yours creep me out."

"Oh, I can fix that," I said. "Do you want to see?"

"Why do I think I'm going to regret this?"

"It's not scary," I assured her. "It's called biological alteration. If I take this amulet in my hand and concentrate on being Zane Tracy, I will transform completely."

"Zane Tracy? Who is that?"

"One of my favorite actors from the movies. Didn't you ever see *Teenage Zombie Fighter*? It was made in 1952."

"Even my mother wasn't born in 1952," Cassidy said. "I didn't know they had movies way back then."

"Oh yes, they had great ones. Grandma Wrinkle and I watched them all. I love zombie movies, so Grandma Wrinkle let me choose Zane Tracy's face and body to create my human form."

"Wait, I don't get it," Cassidy said. "You're really Zane Tracy?"

"No, but my skin is."

Apparently, this was too much for Cassidy. "I have to go," she said, heading for the door. "I don't want to see your face blow up and splatter all over the walls."

"Please stay," I begged. "You'll see how it works. And you'll see that I am still me inside, no matter what I look like on the outside."

"Okay, but I reserve the right to leave if this gets too nauseating."

Cautiously, Cassidy leaned against the wall, close to the door. She was ready to bolt at any second. I took hold of the amulet around my neck and closed my eyes, forcing myself to focus. My whole friendship with Cassidy depended on this moment.

"*Be Zane,*" I chanted. "*Be Zane now.*"

"You talk to yourself? This is bonkers."

"Shhhh," I said. "Don't say a word. I have to concentrate."

Silently, I repeated the words over and over. I lost touch with the Earth world as I felt the familiar flash of electricity in my body, followed by a tightening sensation on my back and legs. It was my human skin, forming and wrapping itself around my sensory enhancer and moving down my legs all the way to my feet. When I opened my eyes and looked down, I saw two human legs, a pair of big feet, and ten wriggly human toes. My sensory enhancer was tightly tucked away under my human skin. I stood up and took a bow.

"Buddy C. Burger," I said to Cassidy. "All complete and at your service."

Cassidy's mouth was hanging so far open I thought her jaw would touch the carpet. She looked like she might cry, and immediately I regretted my decision to transform in front of her. I should have known that watching biological alteration would be too scary for any earthling.

Before I could utter any kind of explanation, thundering footsteps came pounding down the hall. They were too heavy to be Eloise's, so that meant only one thing. Delores was heading toward us, and she was coming fast.

"Kids! Kids! This is incredible," she shouted, arriving breathlessly. She was holding a phone in one hand and a laptop in the other.

"Buddy, you've gone viral," she said. "That clip from the show, it's taken off like a rocket ship. We're getting hits from kids all around the country. Duane just called. He's already heard from the network executives. They're over the moon about this."

"Which moon is that?" I asked. "There are a hundred and eighty-one natural moons orbiting the planets in this solar system alone."

"Listen to me and stop with the sci-fi jokes, Buddy," Delores said. "We are at a crossroads here in your career and I need to know that you're ready to embrace your future and run with it. Grab the brass ring. Go for the gold."

"Gold? Do you want me wear some of your jewelry?"

"It's a figure of speech, Buddy. I'm talking about the golden egg, the golden ticket, the pot of gold at the end of the rainbow. Are you with me?"

"Actually, as much as I love rainbows, Cassidy and I were just discussing how I can't really stay."

"You're not going anywhere, young man, except up," Delores interrupted. "And you're taking Cassidy with you. Kids, we are sitting on a ratings bonanza. Just look at these comments. 'Love that alien. An alien with attitude, it's about time.'"

I glanced over at Cassidy. She was still looking at my feet.

"I can see it all clearly," Delores was saying. "Buddy, you and Cassidy featured on every teen blog in the country. A lead story on *Entertainment Around the Globe*. Maybe even your own line of clothes. Cassidy, this is what we've dreamed of for so long."

"You mean what *you've* dreamed of," Cassidy muttered.

"Duane said the network wants both of you on the red carpet Monday night when the show airs," Delores said. "Buddy, can you do that?"

"I'll have to oil my suction cups so they don't stick to the carpet or collect lint," I said, thinking aloud.

"Cassidy, only salads for you from now until then," Delores clamored on. "You need to fit into that little black sparkly dress. And as for you, Buddy. Tomorrow we shop. I'll take it from here. I'm calling Rosa in wardrobe now. She's a professional stylist and she'll meet us at the mall and help us create a look for you."

As Delores thundered back down the hall, I could hear her talking to Rosa already, telling her about how she saw me as a combination of a classic hunk, yet with an awkward, almost nerd-like appeal. I understood all the words, but I honestly had no idea what she was talking about.

"So, I guess it looks like you're staying," Cassidy said.

"I can leave quietly by the back door, and your mom won't even hear me," I said. "That is, if you want me to."

"Listen, Buddy, can I be honest with you?" Cassidy asked.

"Always."

"I like you. I like me when I'm with you. When we talk, I don't have to be anything but me, and that feels good."

I felt a little lump in my throat, which was a new feeling. I understood what Cassidy was saying—not just the words part, but the feelings part too.

"What doesn't feel good is knowing that you're not human," she went on. "I'm worried that you're going to declare war on the world or beam me up to your planet or splatter me with ectoplasm."

"First of all," I said, "there is no such thing as ectoplasm. It is only in movies."

"Good. I'm glad to hear that."

"And second of all, I am not here to declare war on the Earth. I have come in peace."

"That's a relief too," Cassidy said.

"And third of all, I can't beam you up to my planet because I can't even go back there myself. I had to run away from the evil Squadron, and if they ever find me, they will capture me and deactivate my sensory enhancer."

"You mean that snorty thing on your back?"

"Yes."

"Sounds like a good idea to me."

"Trust me, it's not. The sensory enhancer is what makes us able to feel and sense things deeply, to hear music and see art and cry at movies. Without it, we'd just be robots."

"Is that why you came here, so you wouldn't be turned into a robot?"

"Exactly."

Cassidy thought for a long time.

"What do you say, Cass?" I said, almost too afraid to ask

the question. "Can I stay? Can you keep my secret? Or will that be too much for you?"

She shook her head. "I still have one question."

Uh-oh. I thought. *Here it comes.*

"How do you get red lint out of your suction cups?" she asked.

She broke up laughing, and I did too, like good friends do.

17

What would you like for breakfast, Buddy?"
Delores asked as I walked into the kitchen the
next morning. "Eloise is having chocolate chip pancakes
with raspberry syrup."

"They're yummy," Eloise said, some purple gooey liquid
dribbling from the side of her mouth.

"I wouldn't know about that," Cassidy chimed in. "I'm
not allowed to have pancakes. I'm having some taste-free
egg whites with broccoli."

"Stop complaining, young lady," Delores said. "It's for
your own good. You'll thank me when they take your picture Monday night and it winds up all over YouTube."

I pulled a chair up to the kitchen table and looked at the
food on the plates. My stomach did another one of its back-
flips. I was going to have to figure out some Earth foods my

body could tolerate, but from the looks of it, breakfast foods were not going to be among them.

"Thanks, Delores," I said, "but I'll just have some water."

There was a pitcher of ice water on the table, so I picked it up and drank it all down in two or three big gulps.

"I think I'll help myself to another one of those," I said.

Eloise stared at me, and for the first time since I'd met her, not a word came out of her mouth. I went to the sink, filled the pitcher with tap water, and chugged that one down too.

"Buddy, we don't drink from the pitcher in this house," Delores said. "It's there for everyone to share."

"Oh, I didn't realize that."

"What are you, from outer space?" Cassidy said. I shot her a piercing glance. Was she blowing my secret already? But then I saw a twinkle in her eye and a smile on her face. She shrugged her shoulders and with a giggle said, "What? I was just kidding."

The water felt good in my body, but I knew I was going to need more to last me for the trip to the mall. Since the pitcher was apparently off-limits, I stuck my head under the faucet and gulped down water until I couldn't drink any more.

"I see we're going to have to work on your manners," Delores said. "And your thirst. What's with that?"

"I like to be well hydrated."

"That's certainly an understatement," Delores answered. "If you keep drinking like that, the entire state of California is going to suffer from a water shortage."

I wouldn't want that to happen, so I made a mental note to keep my water intake to a minimum.

"Okay, ten minutes to get ready, everyone," Delores said, taking Cassidy's plate out from under her while her fork was still in midair. "I've arranged for Rosa to meet us at the mall when it opens."

"Cool, can we go to the Hobby Shack?" Eloise asked. "Daddy said I need to get some miniature planes for our airport."

"You're going to ballet class," Delores said.

"But I hate ballet," Eloise whined. "My teacher says I'm clumsy and that I jump like an elephant, and it's a known fact that elephants can't jump."

"Ballet is good for your posture," Delores said. "And it burns up a lot of calories."

There it was, that word again. Cassidy shot me a glance, as if to say, *What'd I tell you?* Her mother really was a professional calorie counter.

The Fashion Oaks Mall took up an entire city block. There were shops selling everything you could imagine, from baby flip-flops to red paint you put on your lips to chairs that vibrated when you sat in them. We were supposed to meet Rosa in front of the furniture store, and since I was starting to feel a little light-headed, I plopped down in one of those chairs.

"You're going to love this," Cassidy said, pushing the ON button.

The chair started to vibrate, and with it, all the water in my stomach began to churn. You probably know the feeling—like a thousand red beetles were somersaulting around in there, kicking their feet all at once. I was relieved when I saw Rosa hurrying to meet us.

"I've done some preshopping," she said, getting right down to business. "And I've picked out some clothes that I believe will really speak to your fan base, Buddy."

"Talking clothes?" I said. "I wonder what they'll say? I'll bet the pants say, 'No, the zipper goes in front, dummy!'"

Cassidy and Rosa shared a laugh, and I joined in, even though I didn't realize I had said something funny. Delores was the only one who did not laugh. She seemed to really enjoy not laughing.

Rosa led us across the mall, past the toy shop, past the pet store, past the jewelry store displaying its shining precious gems. I recognized several of them as minerals that Citizen Three Lips and I used to dig up on my planet—emeralds, sapphires, and black diamonds. It was odd that what humans wore as decoration, we used as marbles.

When we reached the big store at the end, Rosa led us to the men's department, where there was a salesperson waiting for us.

"Hi, Quinton," Rosa said. "This is Buddy. As I told you, he's heading for stardom and we need to give him a look. He's got a red carpet Monday."

Quinton studied me carefully.

"Is this what you typically wear?" he asked. "White tee shirt and jeans."

"Yes, it's what I typically wear because it's all I have."

"Well, not for long, Buddy. You're in Quinton's world now."

He and Rosa went up and down the aisles, picking out shirts and pants and sweatshirts. Then, with his arms loaded with clothes, he asked me to follow him into a fitting room.

"Ladies, you wait here," he said. "Buddy is going to come and model for us. Oh, and by the way," he said, turning to Cassidy, "I love your show."

"Thank you," Cassidy said. "What's your favorite episode?"

"That's enough, Cassidy," Delores said impatiently. "Let Quinton concentrate on Buddy now. We'll send him a signed picture or something later."

The fitting room walls were covered with mirrors. I looked at myself from head to toe. It was the first time I had seen my Zane Tracy look from every angle. Not to sound conceited, but I looked pretty good. Grandma Wrinkle had done a great job.

I put on everything that Quinton had picked out for me. Tight black jeans rolled up at the cuff, a black tee shirt with I NEED SPACE written in white letters, and over it, a black sweatshirt with a hood. I left the dressing room and came out with the old Zane Tracy swagger, the strut he used when he confronted the zombies in the town square in the classic *Attack of the Killer Zombies*. Unfortunately, my strut was ruined when I tripped on the way out and fell flat on my face. I was still getting used to walking on my new Earth feet, and the skintight jeans didn't help any either.

"What do you think?" I asked the assembled group after I regained my composure.

"What do *you* think?" Quinton asked. "You've got to feel good in your own clothes."

"It's a lot of black," I said. "Do you have anything in pink or orange?"

"You don't mean that," Rosa said. "We're going for a cool look for you, Buddy, and black says cool. It's a statement. And that tee shirt is perfect. 'I need space' says *look but don't touch.*"

"Oh, I thought it meant I need space, as in outer space," I said.

"That's Buddy for you," Cassidy said. "He's got outer space on the brain."

We exchanged a secret smile. I was starting to like this little game of ours.

Quinton had me go back into the fitting room and try on more clothes. A black leather jacket with zippers that lead nowhere, black high-top sneakers with zippers that led nowhere, and a canvas cross-body bag with zippers that led nowhere.

"You're looking very cool," Rosa said. "I think we've got your red carpet look."

"Good," I said. "And I'm helping all the people who make zippers too."

"Great, we'll nominate you for a Nobel Peace Prize," Delores said, "right after you win the Emmy."

"Thank you, Delores. That would be lovely."

"Buddy," Cassidy whispered. "She didn't mean it. She was being sarcastic."

Sarcastic. That was a word I didn't know, so I searched my Earth dictionary and found that sarcasm is when you express something that is the opposite of what you really mean. Why would Delores want to do that? It's hard enough to say what you really mean without having to worry about the opposite of what you really mean. No wonder I was so confused by what she said to me.

Delores and Rosa went to the cash register to pay for the clothes. Cassidy glanced around the floor casually, then suddenly took my arm.

"Beware," she said. "Fans at three o'clock."

I followed Cassidy's eyes and noticed that she was looking at a group of girls who had gathered around the underwear counter, which was covered with statues wearing all different kinds of underpants. The girls were giggling. I smiled too. When you think about it, human underwear is pretty funny to look at, especially the ones they call men's briefs. My Earth dictionary defines "brief" as *of short duration*. And those underpants were definitely short.

"That's him," one of the girls said when she saw me smile at them.

They all started to scream like they had seen an alien. Which they had.

"Hi, alien guy," one of the other girls called out. "We think you're so cute. And Cassidy, we love you too."

"Thank you," Cassidy called as she waved to them. "That's so sweet."

Before I knew it, the girls had made their way over to us, surrounding us and talking all at once.

"I want a picture with you," one of the girls said.

"Me too," they all chimed in.

A few other customers from the store who had been watching the commotion pulled out their phones too. Pretty soon, the original four girls became a crowd of twenty or

thirty people, forming a tight circle around us. They moved in so close that their faces became blurry and they were all screaming at once. I could feel my heart start to beat faster. Even though my three lungs were taking in large gulps of air, I felt short of breath.

"I don't like this," I said to Cassidy.

"It's all part of being a star," she answered. "You have to be nice to your fans."

"But they're scaring me," I said. "They're pushing me. I need to get out of here."

"In a few minutes," she said. "We just need to take a few more pictures."

"No, now," I insisted. I hardly recognized the sound of my own voice. All I knew was that I needed to get away. The screams were echoing in my ears and making them buzz. The people surrounding me took up all the oxygen and made it hard to breathe. The circle they made was getting tighter and tighter. I felt like a caged animal and they were all closing in on me.

And then I passed out.

18

I woke up in my bed in Eloise's room, with Delores hovering over me like a helicopter. She was holding a tray covered with plates of food.

"You have to eat, Buddy," she said. "It takes strength to be a star, and you can't just go around passing out all the time. It's bad for your image."

"I'm sorry," I said. "I don't know what got into me."

"Well, I know what didn't get into you, which is food. I've put together this tray of healthy snacks for you. There's a kale salad, a beet-and-broccoli smoothie, peanut butter on whole wheat, and a tofu burger. I'm taking Cassidy for her voice lesson and then going to pick up Eloise. You stay in bed and eat. I want to see everything on this tray gone when I come back."

After she left, I inspected each dish on the tray. I was already woozy, and the smells coming from that food didn't help. I resolved to try each one though, because I could feel myself growing weaker and weaker and I knew Delores was right.

Here is what I discovered about the Earth foods on my tray.

1. Eating kale is like eating lumber.
2. A beet-and-broccoli smoothie isn't smooth, and it also tastes like lumber.
3. Peanut butter glues your tongue to the roof of your mouth.
4. A tofu burger tastes like fermented sand beetle dung.

After trying each food, I was exhausted and laid my head down on the pillow. Something was annoying me, and when I reached back and felt around, I realized that I was lying on three of my alien eyes. When had those popped out? I grabbed Eloise's pink unicorn hand mirror that was on the bed stand and looked at myself. I was shocked to see that my Zane Tracy face had morphed into my alien face without me even realizing it. My human eyes had been replaced by my rotating eyes, and my fluffy human hair had receded back into my bald, bumpy scalp.

I was transforming without willing it to happen.

Why? This was something Grandma Wrinkle had never mentioned. The only answer was that my life force was dwindling and could no longer maintain my Zane Tracy exterior. I wasn't physically strong enough to hold on to my biological transformation. Hydration alone wasn't the answer. I was going to need food that my body could actually absorb. Not human food, but food that nourished me, like the nutritional wafers we eat on my planet.

The nutritional wafers!

There it was! In my haze, I had forgotten about the one remaining wafer that I had left in my spaceship. If I could only get to it, perhaps that one wafer would sustain me until I figured out what foods I could eat here on Earth.

But as I lay there in bed, I felt too weak and hopeless to even imagine getting to my spaceship. It was only a few miles away on the back lot, but as far as I was concerned, it might just as well have been on Saturn.

19

I don't remember the rest of Saturday clearly, but somehow, I had managed to get myself out of bed. I found myself sitting in a lump on the floor and calling out, "Come in!"

The door creaked open and Cassidy stuck her head in.

"Are you feeling better?" she asked. "It's Sunday. You slept all day and night."

Suddenly, the door burst all the way open and Eloise pushed past Cassidy and came bounding in. She looked at me and shrieked.

"Everybody run!" she screamed. "There's an alien in my bedroom!"

"Calm down, shrimp," Cassidy said. "It's Buddy, he's just wearing his costume for the show. Are you afraid of a costume? That's so babyish."

Eloise didn't seem altogether comfortable with Cassidy's explanation, but at least she stopped screaming. Then one of the sour purple gummy dragons detached itself from the ceiling and fell on her head.

"It's raining candy!" she giggled in a sudden change of attitude. She seemed to forget all about my alien look as she popped the gummy dragon into her mouth. It's amazing the effect one gummy dragon can have on an Earth child.

"We need to talk," I whispered to Cassidy. "Alone."

She nodded and turned to Eloise.

"Buddy and I need to go over our lines for tomorrow's rehearsal," she said. "We need you to leave."

"Okay," Eloise said. "But if any more candy falls from the ceiling, call me right away."

When she was gone, I motioned for Cassidy to sit down next to me. I had so little energy, I could barely talk. In a raspy voice, I said, "I'm sick."

"Do you have some weird alien disease that's going to wipe out all of humanity?" she asked.

"Not that kind of sick." I shook my head. "Hungry sick. I need food. Like the nutritional wafers from my planet."

"Well, we don't have any of those, but we do have Ritz crackers. I could put some peanut butter on them."

Cassidy pushed herself up from the floor and headed for the door.

"No, I need to get the nutritional wafer that's in my spaceship."

She stopped walking and turned to me, a surprised look on her face. "What spaceship?"

"The one I came here in. I didn't come by subway."

"So where is this spaceship? In a crater in the middle of the desert?"

"It's on the back lot. In between the churro cart and the burger stand."

Cassidy crouched down and looked me square in the face. "Wait, are you telling me you just flew to Earth and parked your spaceship in the middle of the biggest tourist attraction in Los Angeles and no one noticed? That's bizarre."

"Everyone on the tour thinks it's a prop from a movie. Even Luis."

"I get that. The attractions on the tour are very convincing. When I was little, I thought those dinosaurs were real. I was so scared until my dad told me that my room had an invisible force field that kept the dinosaurs out."

"A force field? Was it electromagnetic or atomic?"

"It was imaginary, silly."

She laughed, but I didn't have the energy to join in. The best I could manage was a weak nod of the head. Cassidy looked concerned.

"You poor thing," she said. "We have to get to your spaceship. I could ask my mom to drive us, but she's so nosy, she'd ask a million questions."

"I can call Luis and ask him to come pick me up. He's been a good friend to me."

I tried to stand up, but crumbled back down into a heap. Cassidy took me by the arm and helped me to my feet so I could get a good grip on the floor with my suction cups.

"Looks like we're going together," she said. "You're in no shape for a solo expedition."

When we called Luis, he didn't answer right away. When he finally did, he sounded rushed.

"What's up, Buddy?" he said. "Make it fast, dude, because I'm in the middle of work."

"I need a favor, Luis. Can you come pick me up at Cassidy's and take me to the back lot? I need to get something from that spaceship."

"Dude, I am working. I got twenty kids around me right now. Three of them are trying to hang on to my neck bolts, and the rest are waiting for a Frankenstein selfie."

"I wouldn't bother you except that this is a matter of life and death," I told him.

"Okay, okay, no need to be so melodramatic, dude. I got a break coming up in twenty minutes. Text me the address and I'll shoot right over." Then I heard the squeals of little kids through the phone and Luis saying, "Hey, little man, touch that bolt again and my head is going to fall off right in your lap."

Twenty minutes later, with Cassidy holding me up, we snuck through the house, headed for the driveway to wait for Luis. But nothing escapes Delores, and she cornered me as we opened the front door.

"What's with the costume, Buddy?" she asked.

"I like to wear it on the weekend sometimes. It keeps me in character for the show. It's something we actors do."

"'We actors?'" Delores said, rolling her eyes. "Wow, it didn't take you long to become Mr. Hollywood."

When Luis pulled into the driveway, he got out of his faded red convertible and opened the passenger door for us. He was wearing his green Frankenstein suit with the giant platform boots, but his Frankenstein head was strapped into the back seat with a seat belt. Delores looked him up and down.

"What's with you guys? Do you think every day is Halloween?" she asked.

"These are my work clothes," Luis answered.

"You better put that top up," she said. "If the cops see you, they'll think you've both lost it."

Suddenly, a piercing shriek shot through the air. It was Eloise, who had wandered outside to see who had pulled up.

"A green monster with a human face!" she screamed. "It's not getting me."

She ran back into the house and slammed the door. Luis just chuckled. "I consider that a compliment," he said.

We got into the car and pulled out of the driveway, leaving the top down. I breathed deeply and let the fresh air fill all three of my lungs. Once we arrived on the Universal back lot, Luis parked in staff parking and we agreed to meet him there in fifteen minutes. With Cassidy supporting my limp body, we hurried past the throngs of tourists who were all snapping pictures. When we got to the door of the spaceship, I was too weak to climb up the stairs myself. Cassidy helped me and opened the hatch so I could crawl in.

"Maybe you should wait here," I said to her.

"No deal," she answered. "This is my chance to be on *Star Trek*, but for real."

I climbed inside the spaceship and Cassidy followed.

"Watch your head," I warned. "It's tight quarters in here."

I took my place in the pilot's chair as Cassidy wedged herself into the passenger seat. Urgently, I pushed the silver button that opened the compartment on the dashboard where the nutritional wafers were supposed to be. The compartment lid popped open but there was nothing inside. My heart sank. I didn't remember having eaten all the wafers, but the compartment was definitely empty.

"Oh," Cassidy said. "I'm sitting on something."

She reached down and pulled a silver-wrapped package out from under her. It contained the last nutritional wafer, which I must have tossed on the seat in my haste to get to my studio identification picture.

I snatched the package from Cassidy's hand, ripped it open, and the wafer slid out. Before I could catch it, it slipped down into the crack between our seats. I stuck my spiny fingers into the crevice to retrieve it, but my long fingernails got ensnared by all the wiring and couldn't reach the wafer. It had been over a day since I had trimmed my nails, and they had grown several inches in that time.

"Help!" I said weakly. "Cassidy, it's up to you."

She tried to put her hand down into the crack, but it didn't fit. Human hands are too pudgy.

"I have to find something small enough to get in there," she said, looking frantically around the cabin. There was nothing. Then she caught sight of the amulet around my neck.

"I can use that," she said. "I'll attach this piece of gum I'm chewing to the end of it. Then I'll drop it down, your wafer will stick to it, and I'll pull it up. Just like going fishing."

"You can't touch this amulet," I said, grasping it and holding it tightly to my chest.

"Why, are you afraid I'm going to borrow your jewelry and not give it back?"

"It's not jewelry," I said. "It contains the titanium vial that allows me to biologically alter. If anything happens to this amulet, I'm toast. Or maybe even just the crumbs left behind by toast."

"Buddy, you have to trust me," she said. "We don't have any other options."

She reached over and took the amulet from around my neck. Taking the wad of gum from her mouth, she attached it carefully to the tip, then lowered the chain into the crack between our chairs. Her face was all concentration as she slowly moved it around in the dark crevice.

"Got it," she said. "Now I just hope it sticks."

I stuck my longest fingernail into the crevice until it found the wad of gum. Gently, I pressed it against the wafer, trying to increase the bond between them.

"That's the best I can do," I said.

"Okay, here goes. I'm reeling it in."

She pulled on the chain ever so gently, and little by little, the wafer made its way up through the crevice. As soon as it emerged, I couldn't resist another second. I bent down and chomped off a big hunk, swallowing it in one gulp while making sure I didn't eat the amulet. As I tried to gobble down the rest of it, Cassidy pulled the wafer away from me.

"You can't finish it," she said. "We need to save a piece so we can figure out what's in it. Then we'll know what you can eat."

I was so hungry I could have eaten an entire asteroid belt. I wanted every bite of that wafer, but realized that Cassidy was completely right.

"You're so smart," I said, and she smiled.

Immediately, I started to feel better. My head fog cleared up, my limbs grew strong, and my suction cups puckered tightly on the spaceship floor. Whatever was in that wafer was exactly the nourishment my body needed. Seeing that I was coming back to life, Cassidy handed the amulet back to me, and I carefully placed it around my neck. We both knew this was something I could never lose. My life depended on it.

"We still have five minutes before we have to meet Luis," Cassidy said. "Why don't you show me all the cool alien stuff you've got in here?"

It felt really good that Cassidy was accepting the real me. I liked that she was curious about my other life.

"I can show you the coolest thing ever," I said, "if you promise it won't freak you out. It's really special to me."

"Bring it on," Cassidy said. "I want to see what's special to you."

I pushed the silver button on the dashboard, the one that popped open the compartment that held the mini-projector.

"Begin now," I commanded.

The hologram of Grandma Wrinkle appeared and filled the cabin.

"If you are watching this," she said, just as she had said the first time I played that hologram, "then I know your journey is complete and you have arrived safely."

"Who is that old woman?" Cassidy asked softly.

"My grandmother," I said, tears forming in four of my six eyes.

"You must really miss her," Cassidy said.

"She is the most important person in my life. She sacri-ficed so much for me. She may be in terrible danger at this very minute."

"I'm so sorry, Buddy," Cassidy said. "You'll see her again. I know you will."

I shook my head. I didn't see how that was possible.

"I feel so far away and alone," I said, tears flowing from all six of my eyes now.

"You're not alone," Cassidy said, taking my spiny hand in hers. "You have me."

We sat there, listening to Grandma Wrinkle speak. At the sound of her voice, my sensory enhancer came alive and reached out to her, making kissing sounds. I felt the same way. I wanted to throw my arms around her and hold on to her forever. But I knew she wasn't really there, that she was just a hollow image made of nothing but beams of fleeting light.

20

The nutritional wafer gave me enough energy to make it through the rest of the day. When we got home from my spaceship, I transformed back into Zane Tracy because once Eloise got used to seeing me in "my costume," she kept asking me to rotate my eyes, which was really annoying.

"Put your cool costume back on," she said. "I want to see you do that buggy-eye trick again."

"We have important grown-up stuff to do here," Cassidy told her. "You're bothering us."

"All you're doing is staring at that cookie," Eloise said. "What's so grown-up about that?"

We had sat down at the kitchen table with the remainder of the nutritional wafer in front of us. Cassidy kept it close to her for fear I was going to grab it and scarf it down, which I was very tempted to do.

"Eloise," Cassidy said, "be a good girl and go get the magnifying glass from the drawer in Dad's desk."

"I wish Dad were here so he could get it himself," Eloise said.

I felt so bad for her that I decided next time I transformed I would give her a real treat and show her everything my eyes can do. Not only do they rotate around my head, but the actual eyeballs can spin inside their sockets. I hoped that would cheer her up.

Cassidy broke off a tiny piece of the wafer and held it up to the light.

"What do you see?" I asked.

"Brown junk."

"That's not a very scientific analysis."

"Okay," Cassidy said. "Brown molecules. Is that better?"

Eloise returned with the magnifying glass, and Cassidy and I inspected the piece of the wafer. All the magnifying glass did was make the little piece bigger, but it didn't show us any of the ingredients.

"I'm going in for a taste," Cassidy said. "Maybe I can identify what's in it. You don't think this is going to make me grow six eyes, do you?"

"That would really be something to see."

"Here goes nothing," she said. Then she leaned in close to me and whispered, "I've never eaten anything from outer space before."

She placed a little bit of the wafer on her tongue and closed her eyes.

"What do you taste?" I asked.

"It's strange. I know the human tongue has over eight thousand taste buds, but not one of mine is reporting in. It isn't sour or sweet or salty or bitter. It tastes like nothing."

"It's designed that way," I explained. "The Supreme Leader wants to make sure all our food is tasteless so we never experience joy. He believes joy leads to rebellion."

"That's a cool story," Eloise said. "Did you just make that up? What happens next?"

"Next you leave the room," Cassidy said. "Like right now."

"But I want to taste that thing too," Eloise said, reaching for the wafer. "I have great taste buds."

Cassidy practically threw her body on top of the wafer to protect it.

"You can never touch this," she said to Eloise. "It's very special. I'm going to put it in a baggie and hold on to it for safekeeping."

"Fine," Eloise said. "You can keep your brown junk. I'd rather have a tangerine popsicle anyway."

She went to the freezer, grabbed a popsicle, and ran off to annoy someone else.

"Now what?" I asked. "I wish we were on my planet, where we have top scientists like my grandmother who can analyze any problem and come up with a solution."

"We have plenty of scientists here on Earth," Cassidy said. "I just don't happen to know any. I know art directors and actors and costume designers. The closest person I know to a scientist is Janice, our set teacher. Sometimes we do units on science. Ulysses really loves them, but Tyler hates science because he says it makes his brain hurt."

"What brain?" I asked. That made Cassidy laugh.

We got Janice's number from the crew list and called her. Cassidy explained that we wanted to do a scientific experiment that analyzed the ingredients in food.

"Is this your mother trying to get you to count calories again?" Janice asked. "I wish she'd get off your back."

"Why do you say that?"

"Well, I didn't mention this," Janice said, "but last month, your mother ordered a food analysis kit and asked if I could run a test on a diet chocolate pudding. Apparently, you had just discovered it and she didn't trust the label, which said it was only fifty calories."

Cassidy frowned so hard it seemed like her face was shrinking into itself.

"I can't believe she did that," she said softly into the phone.

"Don't worry, Cass," Janice said. "I didn't do it. I advised her that it's better for you to eat nutritionally, like your body tells you to."

"Wait a minute," I said to Janice. "I'm sorry to interrupt, but did you say you had a food analysis kit? Do you still have it?"

"Probably," she answered. "I tossed it into one of the drawers in my desk."

"We need to use it," I said. "Could you go get it now?"

Janice laughed. "I love your interest in science, Buddy, but this is Sunday and I'm on my way to the movies. I'll find it tomorrow."

"First thing?" I asked.

"I promise," Janice said. "Always happy to help my students explore the world of science. But someone's going to have to explain to Tyler that this science lesson might require a little thinking. He's not going to take that well."

Cassidy was fuming with anger when we hung up with Janice.

"Can you believe my mother?" she said. "Checking up on me behind my back."

"It's good that Janice didn't go along with it," I said. "I'm sure your mother thinks she's doing what's best for you."

"Yeah, well, maybe she should consult me on that. It's my life."

I felt so bad for her. I was lucky that Grandma Wrinkle never tried to make me into anything I wasn't. She always listened to me and tried to help me become a better me.

"Can I get you a tangerine popsicle?" I offered. That had seemed to cheer Eloise up.

"That's sweet, Buddy," she said. "You're sweet. At least we understand each other."

"We're a good team," I agreed.

"You bet we are," she said. "Look what we did with Janice. We had a problem and we solved it. I can't wait for tomorrow, so we can get you fed so you'll be strong for the red carpet."

I didn't have the heart to tell her that we hadn't really solved the problem. At that very minute, the tips of my human toes were starting to shrivel, and I could feel my life force wane again. I wanted to lie down and sleep, but I didn't dare. My body was telling me that it needed the right nutrition. The clock was ticking.

Before bed, I transformed back into my alien self, because I thought being in my natural state might take up less of my life force. I tried soaking in the tub for a few hours, and that helped some, but by morning I was very light-headed as Delores drove us to the studio.

When we got to Stage 42, Cassidy and I looked around for Janice, but she wasn't there yet. Duane said she had called in to say she'd be late because of car trouble.

"Exactly how late?" I demanded. There was an unpleasant urgency in my voice, which I couldn't mask.

"Easy does it, Buddy," Duane snapped. "Janice doesn't work for you."

"I didn't mean to be rude," I said. "It's just that I'm dying to get some science information and my quest for knowledge is in high gear."

"Typical," Tyler grunted. "Goes along with the rest of your nerdy self. By the way, why'd you wear your costume to work?"

I didn't have a ready answer, but Cassidy stepped in to help me out.

"Buddy wants to stay in character as much as possible," she said. "It's called acting, Tyler. You should try it."

As we gathered for the table read to go over the new script, Ulysses congratulated me on all the attention I had gotten over the weekend and Martha sang me a wonderful song called "Celebration." Tyler stood sullenly by, just watching. While everyone was getting seated, he swaggered up to me and whispered in my ear.

"Hey, runt, if I were you, which I'm glad I'm not, I'd be careful of social media. It's easy to become the flavor of the day. The real test is if you're still popular a few weeks from now."

I didn't have the energy to come up with a response, so I just nodded and thanked him for the advice.

"It's not advice, doof," he said. "It's a warning. I'll still be standing when you're down for the count. You can trust me on that."

"Good morning, everyone," Duane began as we settled in around the table. "We are happy to welcome our newest permanent cast member, Buddy Burger. Buddy, you created quite a stir this weekend. I think you're going to be really good for our show."

Everyone cheered and applauded. Everyone, that is, but a certain dark-haired, handsome teen idol named Tyler Stone.

"In this week's episode, we learn that Buddy's alien intelligence wins him a scholarship to Oddball Academy," Duane said. "I'm going to need everyone's cooperation in rehearsal because we have a short day today. You all know that the network is throwing us a red carpet party tonight on the back lot just before the show airs. It's in Buddy's honor. What do you think of that, Buddy?"

"Actually, my favorite color is yellow," I said. "Can they make it a yellow carpet?"

Everyone laughed, which I didn't understand until Cassidy tugged on my arm and whispered to me. "It's a red carpet *event*. With photographers and press and fans all lining up to get a look at you. You're going to get to walk the red carpet, every TV star's dream."

As I listened to her explanation, I felt my head spin, and then the whole world flipped upside down. Was that nerves from the realization that all the human world would be watching me on the red carpet? Or was my life force dipping even lower? Janice still hadn't shown up, and my need for food was getting urgent. If I didn't get some nutrition soon, the only place I was going to be walking was into a hospital. Or worse.

Maybe water would help. In desperation, I picked up my glass of water on the table and drank it down. Then I reached for Cassidy's and drank that too. Martha offered me hers, and so did Ulysses. I finished theirs in two gulps. Tyler stared at me suspiciously.

"You must be half camel," he said.

"Actually, he's the opposite of a camel," Ulysses said. "Camels don't need water. They can survive for six months in the desert."

"Where'd you learn that?" Tyler said.

"It's a little thing called a book," Ulysses answered.

"You might try opening one sometime," Martha added. Then she and Ulysses high-fived each other while Tyler just sneered at them. They seemed like such good friends, and I liked them a lot.

"Enough of this chitchat, kids," Duane said. "Let's get started. Everyone please turn to page one, Interior Oddball Academy cafeteria."

I held the script up to my forehead to memorize it. I could feel that the words on the page were not flowing into me. It was as if a guard were standing at the entrance to my brain with a DO NOT ENTER sign.

We began the script reading. With the help of six more glasses of water, I was able to stumble through it. Mary brought me my own pitcher of water.

"Here you go, honey," she said. "You seem parched. Nerves will do that to you. You don't want to get cotton mouth."

Duane took notes as we read the script, giving occasional suggestions for line readings. About halfway through, there was a really funny scene in the cafeteria where Ulysses is talking as Albert Einstein.

"Even zo I am zee greatest scientist to ever live," he said, "and have solved all zee unsolvable mysteries of zee universe, I cannot for mine life figure out what is zis mystery meat zey are serving today in zee cafeteria."

Everyone laughed at his Albert Einstein accent, including Ulysses himself. The laughter was so loud that no one noticed when Duane's phone started to buzz with a text. No one but me, that is.

Duane looked at the screen.

"Sorry to interrupt the fun," he said, "but I have to answer this message. It's Janice, and she says she's got a problem."

He got up and left the table.

I never took my eyes off him as he read the message on his phone. If Janice had a problem, then I did too.

21

When Duane returned to the table reading, he said nothing about the text from Janice. The minute we had finished the script, I practically flew over to him.

"What did Janice say?" I asked him.

"Busted fan belt."

"Is that anything like an asteroid belt?"

Duane put his arm around my shoulders and gave me a serious look.

"Let me give you a tip, Buddy. If you keep insisting on staying in this alien character, you're going to burn yourself out, not to mention annoy all your fellow castmates. A little bit of alien goes a long way."

"Okay. But can you just tell me how long it takes to fix a busted fan belt?"

"Depends if they have the right one in stock," he said.

"Oh, she said to tell you that what you're looking for is in the bottom drawer of her desk."

I whipped around and headed to the back of the soundstage where Janice had a desk and some tables and chairs set up as our informal classroom.

"Not so fast," Duane called after me. "I need you onstage to rehearse. You're in the opening scene. Cassidy's waiting for you on the cafeteria set."

"But this isn't a good time for me," I protested.

Tyler had overheard the conversation.

"What'd I tell you, Duane?" he said. "Give this no-talent one little break, and he's already got a star attitude." Then, turning to me, he said, "On set, we do what the director says, doof. You better get that through your bald alien head."

I managed to get through the rehearsal of the opening scene, although I did bump into every piece of furniture on the set. Cassidy was really helpful. She could see I was struggling, and every time I lost my balance, she'd reach out to steady me.

"Hang in there, Buddy," she whispered. "Just a few more minutes."

Luckily, neither of us was in the next scene, so we were free to go. We raced to the classroom, and I pulled open the bottom drawer of Janice's desk. I didn't find anything that looked like a food analysis kit.

"She said it was in the bottom drawer," I said as I continued to rummage around.

"Here, let me look." Cassidy pushed me aside, which wasn't hard to do because my suction cups didn't have much grip left in them. Moving a stack of index cards, Cassidy pulled out a cardboard box that said FOOD ANALYSIS KIT.

"It was right here all along, Buddy."

That was alarming. I had looked directly at it and not seen it. My eyes, at least several of them, were failing.

We sat down at the table and opened the box. It contained about thirty glass vials, fifteen dropper bottles with different-colored solutions, and an instruction manual.

"Here," Cassidy said, handing me the manual. "Put this up to your forehead and absorb it. Tell me what it says."

I held the manual to my forehead, but once again, the information was having trouble getting through. Words were coming in, but not in the right order—*sugar, lipids, analytical methods, amino acids.* None of it made sense to me.

"We're running out of time," I said. "We'll just have to figure this out on our own."

"It seems pretty logical," Cassidy said. "We put a little bit of the wafer into each of these glass vials. Then we put drops of all the different solutions into each vial. Let's get a knife and cut the wafer up."

There was no need for a knife. My fingernails, which hadn't been trimmed in two days and had grown out of control, were sharper than knives. I broke off little pieces of wafer and Cassidy put one piece in each vial with several drops of solution.

Then we waited. And waited. And waited. Nothing happened. We just stared at those little glass vials. I was concentrating so hard on the vials that I nearly jumped ten feet in the air when Jules the stage manager appeared and touched my shoulder.

"Buddy, Duane needs you for the next scene," he said.

"Could you tell him I'm really busy?" I asked.

"Sure, I can tell him that," Jules said. "And then I can pack my things because I'll be fired."

"You go," Cassidy said to me. "I'll stay here and watch these. I'll let you know if anything changes."

I followed Jules to the set, but my mind stayed with the vials. The scene we were rehearsing was when Tyler discovers that he and the alien are going to be roommates.

INT. DORMITORY ODDBALL ACADEMY — DAY

Tyler is lying on his bunk bed, watching TV. Buddy the alien enters.

                    TYLER
         Hey, space creep, you're supposed
         to knock when you come in someone's
         room.

BUDDY THE ALIEN

Even if it's my own room?

TYLER

This is *my* room.

BUDDY THE ALIEN

Correction. *Was* your room. Now it's
our room. Or as I like to call it,
my biosphere.

TYLER

Tell me you're not actually going
to be my roommate.

BUDDY THE ALIEN

I brought my personal robot. His
name is ZR 733. He's very nice, except he snores. He'll stop if you
just put your finger up his nose.

TYLER

Up his nose? No, this is NOT happening. I'm going to talk to Principal Broadbottom.

BUDDY THE ALIEN

Great, I'll come with you. I'd like to get to know Principal Broadbottom better.

Tyler and I rehearsed the scene. I was able to get through it, even though my tongue was feeling heavy and my lips thick. The one thing I couldn't do was pronounce Principal Broadbottom's name. No matter how hard I tried, it kept coming out Principal Dogbottom or Principal Waddlebottom. The crew thought that was funny. Duane didn't.

"Concentrate, Buddy," he snapped. "We aren't rehearsing just for fun. This is a movie studio, not a kindergarten."

I finally got it right, and Duane moved on to the next scene, which didn't involve me. Cassidy was standing on the sideline, motioning for me to come with her.

"It's amazing," she said, taking my hand and pulling me back to the classroom. "Every vial has changed color. I looked in the manual and it tells you what nutrient each color stands for. Buddy, you're going to be eating real space food soon."

At the table, we got out a notebook and started to compare each color to what was in the manual.

"A greenish color indicates copper," Cassidy read from the book.

I wrote down *copper* in the notebook.

"Yellow indicates potassium," Cassidy read.

One of the vials was definitely bright yellow.

"The presence of vitamin K will be indicated by a purple color."

As Cassidy read off the colors we had, I took notes until we had a complete list of all the ingredients. I won't bore you with the whole list, but it included niacin and folate; vitamins A, B6, C, and K; and calcium, magnesium, and a whole lot of other hard-to-pronounce minerals.

"This is great," Cassidy said. "Now we know exactly what you need to eat. All we have to do is find an Earth food that matches this list."

"How do we do that?" I asked.

"Well, there's this handy-dandy thing called the internet," Cassidy said. "You ever heard of that in outer space?"

"Yes," I said. "We learned about it in ancient history class."

"You're such a show-off," Cassidy said with a smile. "Wait here while I go do some research on my laptop."

While I sat at the classroom table, Martha, Tyler, and Ulysses came to see what was going on.

"What's all this garbage?" Tyler asked, looking at the vials of colored solution.

"Cassidy and I were doing a science experiment," I said. "Analyzing the nutritional content of food."

"Boring!" he said. "Why don't you just open your mouth and eat like normal people do? Oh, I forgot. You don't have teeth."

"I love science," Ulysses said. "Let's try your experiment on other foods."

"Count me out," Tyler said. "If you need me, I'll be in my dressing room trying out new hair gel."

Tyler sauntered off. Martha was munching on a snack she called Pop Rocks, which as far as I could see were bright red little candy kernels that sizzled when you put them in your mouth.

"Now, there's a science experiment waiting to happen," Ulysses said.

He grabbed a few of the Pop Rocks from Martha's bag and tossed them into one of the vials. Immediately, the water turned hot pink and started to sizzle. A plume of steam rose from the vial, emitting a strong, sweet odor.

"Mmmm," Martha said. "Watermelon."

I felt my sensory enhancer sit up and take notice of the fruity fragrance. Its trunk circled the air, snorting with pleasure. Martha burst out laughing.

"I don't know how you rigged that thing up, Buddy," she said, "but it's the funniest costume I've ever seen."

"You can tell us, dude," Ulysses said. "Is it battery operated or what?"

My brain was too tired to come up with a story, so I heard myself saying, "It's an alien secret. This is my sensory enhancer, and if I told you all about it, the Squadron would come from my planet and arrest me."

"And then little green men would kidnap us in their spaceship and take us to your planet," Ulysses said, with a grin.

He and Martha were still laughing when Cassidy came running up.

"Hey, Cass," Ulysses said. "Join the fun. Buddy was just telling us that he really is an alien."

Cassidy laughed right along with them.

"That Buddy," she said. "He's always joking. Now, can you

guys leave us alone for a second? I have something important to tell him."

"Sure," Ulysses laughed. "Just watch out for the little green men."

Ulysses and Martha left. Cassidy grabbed me by the shoulders, a big smile spreading across her face.

"I found it," she said. "I found the food you need."

"What is it?"

"Are you sitting down?"

"Why? Do I look like I'm sitting down?"

"It's avocado," she said. I stared at her blankly. "It's a fruit," she added.

I had never heard of it. In movies, I'd seen humans eating all kinds of fruit—apples, bananas, oranges, grapes, pineapples, berries, and watermelon. But never an avocado.

I put the word "avocado" through my Earth dictionary and came up with this definition: *a pear-shaped fruit with rough bumpy skin, smooth edible flesh, and a large stone in the middle.*

That certainly didn't sound delicious. But I was desperate, willing to try anything. We had the red carpet event coming up in less than six hours, and I was feeling so weak I couldn't imagine attending.

"Where can we get these leathery avocado fruits?" I asked.

"I looked for Mary to see if she had any, but I couldn't find her. Jules said she had to go pick up her kid at school."

"So, what do we do now?" I asked.

"Don't worry. I have it all worked out," Cassidy said. "I'm going to take you to the one place we'll be sure to find avocados. We're going to see the true America."

"We're going to the Mississippi River?"

"No, silly," she laughed.

"The Rocky Mountains?"

"Nope."

"Then where?"

"Buddy, my alien friend, we're going to the supermarket."

22

We told Delores that we were going to spend our lunch hour with Luis. She wasn't happy about that.

"You should be studying your lines," she told Cassidy. "Stars aren't born, you know. They're made, with plenty of—"

"Hard work and dedication," Cassidy said in unison with her mother. I could tell she had heard that speech plenty of times.

"Don't be gone long," Delores warned, "because as soon as Duane dismisses you, we're going to hot roller your hair for tonight. And squeeze you into that little black dress. You too, Buddy."

"Thank you, but I don't look good in dresses."

"You know what I mean, smarty-pants. We've got to prep you too. Tonight is the night that Buddy Burger tells the world 'HERE I AM!' Are you ready?"

I couldn't have been less ready.

Cassidy had already called Luis and asked him if he could take us out on his lunch hour. She wouldn't tell him where, but she promised it would be fun.

"Hey, I love a mystery," he said. "And I love fun. And I love you guys. So consider that a yes."

Luis drove his old convertible right up to the stage door and we climbed in. As usual, he had his Frankenstein suit on, except for the head, which was strapped into the back seat.

"I got forty-seven minutes before I have to be back at work," he said. "Where are we going?"

"To the supermarket," Cassidy said.

Luis stopped the car.

"I thought you said this was going to be fun," he complained. "No offense, kids, but cruising down the tuna fish aisle is not my idea of a hot time."

"No tuna, I promise," Cassidy said. "We're in the market for avocados."

"Oh, now there's something I know all about," Luis said. "My grandmother goes through crates of them every week to make her world-famous guacamole. People line up around the block at her restaurant."

"What's guacamole?" I asked. I remembered Luis mentioning it once, but I had never bothered to run it through my Earth dictionary.

"You must be from outer space, dude, if you don't know what guacamole is. It's only the best food on the planet. It's a game changer for your tongue."

"But we need avocados, not guacamole," I said.

"Guacamole is mashed avocado," Luis said. "Add lime juice, some salt, maybe tomatoes or garlic, plus a heaping tablespoon of Grandma Lupe's love, and you have a snack fit for a king."

I felt a sharp pain in my left leg, like a really bad cramp. Even my leg muscles were demanding food. I let out a little moan. I didn't intend to, but it just fell out of my mouth.

"How fast can you get us to the market?" Cassidy asked.

"Man, you guys aren't messing around," Luis said as he pulled out of the main gate and waved to Scotty the guard. "I'm on it. When your taste buds call, Luis answers."

We drove down Ventura Boulevard, passing rows of sushi restaurants that looked like little wooden Japanese houses.

"I love sushi," Cassidy said. "Do you, Luis?"

"I could eat it all day long. How about you, Buddy? A slab of raw tuna, or maybe a giant clam? I like it when it's still pulsating. Puts hair on your chest."

I was already feeling queasy, and the idea of eating a raw fish or, worse, an uncooked mollusk, made my stomach do a flip-flop. I put my head between my knobby knees and kept it there until we pulled into the parking lot of Valu-Rite Super Market.

"I'll get us a cart," Cassidy said, climbing out of the back seat. While she was wheeling the cart over to us, I was immediately spotted by a little boy riding in the baby seat of his mother's cart.

"Look, a space man," he yelled, pointing at me with his chubby finger. "And a monster," he screamed again when he saw Luis behind me. "Mommy, can we buy them?"

His mother didn't look surprised to see us. She just smiled and took a sip of her iced coffee.

"You guys must be on break from Universal Studios," she said. "And you're Cassidy from *Oddball Academy*. My daughters love the show. Could you take a picture with us? They'll be so excited."

"The spaceman too," the little boy screamed.

She handed Luis the phone and I climbed out of the car for the picture. I hung on to the side of her cart to stabilize myself. I had the horrible feeling that the Earth was rotating but I wasn't rotating with it. When I let go of the cart, I practically crumbled into a heap.

"I need to ride in the cart," I said weakly.

"Dude, that is too weird," Luis said. "You never know when there's going to be a photographer around to snap your picture."

Once we got inside the market, at least ten people pointed and said, "Look, there's that cute alien everyone's talking about."

All I could do was smile weakly and spin an eyeball or two at them.

Cassidy pushed me to the fruit-and-vegetable department and stopped in front of the avocado display. She picked up several avocados and squeezed them.

"You're hurting them," I said.

"Fruits and vegetables don't have feelings."

"How do you know? Why do you think lemons are so sour? They must have had terrible childhoods."

"Well, even if they did it doesn't matter now, because the only way I can tell if these avocados are ripe is to squeeze them. They're supposed to be soft. These ones are hard as bricks."

We asked the produce man if they had any ripe avocados, but he said they were out. All we could do was wait a few days for these ones to ripen.

"I don't have a few days," I told him.

"Why, you got a hot dinner date on the moon?" he asked. "Watch out, because I hear that place has no atmosphere."

There were two reasons I didn't laugh at his joke. One was because it wasn't funny. And two was because I thought I was literally dying. My vision was getting fuzzy and my sensory enhancer hadn't moved for hours.

Even though they weren't ripe, Cassidy insisted that we load our cart with every single avocado on the table. There must have been two hundred of them, wedged around me until all you could see was my head sticking out. When we got to the counter, the checkout woman raised an eyebrow.

"Let's see," she said. "You have seventy-five pounds of avocados, and one alien." Then, with a twinkle in her eye, she picked up her microphone and said, "Joe, I need a price check on aliens."

I thought if one more person made a joke, I might literally pass away right there in the market. Cassidy must have seen the desperation on my face, because she got all businesslike with the checkout woman.

"If you don't mind, we're really in a big hurry," Cassidy said.

"You're just like my husband," the woman said. "He doesn't appreciate my sense of humor either."

She rang up all the avocados and Luis put them in bags. It was such a relief to finally escape the supermarket . . . and all the jokers inside.

Luis drove us back to Stage 42 and helped Cassidy carry the bags of avocados to my dressing room.

"You better not eat those things until they're ripe," he warned, "or you'll have a major tummy ache. And stay away from the pits and the skin. They can be poisonous."

I nodded, but inside, I knew I was going to have to risk it.

"Am I invited to your red carpet event tonight?" Luis asked. "I hear it's going to be fantastic."

"Of course you can come," Cassidy said. "In fact, why don't you meet us here at six o'clock. You can ride in our limo."

"You don't have to ask me twice." Luis grinned. "This will be my first time in a limo. Luis Rivera, livin' his best life."

Then he flashed me a thumbs-up and left.

"I can't go tonight," I told Cassidy. "I can barely breathe, even though I have three lungs."

"I'm going to go find Mary," she said. "She must be back by now. Maybe she has something with avocado in it, to tide you over until these things ripen."

The minute she was gone, I dove for the avocados in the grocery bags. I squeezed every one of them, trying to find one that was even a little ripe. They were hard as nails. I tried to use my razor-sharp fingernails to puncture the skin, but they were no match for the leathery avocado. In desperation, I took a bite of one anyway, but having no teeth put me at a distinct disadvantage. I couldn't pry off any flesh. All I was able to get were little bits of the bitter black rind. Then I remembered Luis's warning, that eating avocado skin could be poisonous. I spit it out the second it hit my tongues.

(In case I hadn't mentioned this before, I have two tongues, an upper one and a lower one.)

When Cassidy came back, she had Mary with her.

"Good news," she said. "Look what Mary has dug up."

Mary held out a little plastic cup with a couple spoonfuls of a mushy green substance.

"Guacamole," she said. "It's all that's left from our taco lunch today, but Cassidy said any amount would do."

I snatched the cup from her hand, stuck out my tongue, being careful to use only my upper tongue so as not to freak Mary out, and licked the cup clean.

"That's right," Mary said. "Everyone says my guacamole is good to the last drop."

"Do you have any more?" I asked. "I'm desperate."

"The crew cleaned me out at lunch," she said. "But I'll tell you who probably does. Your pal Luis. I hear his grandmother's restaurant has the best guacamole in Los Angeles. I've never been there myself, but a lot of the crew go there after a show."

"Good idea. We'll try that," Cassidy said as Mary left.

"We should have thought of asking Luis's grandmother back at the market," I said to Cassidy. "What was wrong with us?"

"We didn't think it through," Cassidy answered. "Maybe because you're fainting all over the place and I'm in a total panic trying to save an alien life-form? That can interfere with your thought process, for sure."

"Well, can you call Luis right away?" I asked. "See if he can get some of his grandmother's guacamole over here."

"He's going to be so mad," Cassidy said. "He gave up his whole lunch and now we're asking him another favor."

"It's a matter of life and death," I said weakly.

"Did Mary's guacamole help?" Cassidy asked.

"I don't know, maybe a little. I can see okay out of eyeballs one and six, which were blurry a few minutes ago. But, Cassidy, I can feel my time running out."

Cassidy picked up her phone, and I heard her say, "Hello, Luis. Cass here. Don't hang up. You're not going to believe this, but I have just a teeny-tiny favor to ask."

Then her voice became too far away for me to make out the words. Suddenly, I felt a swirl of electrical current under my skin, like the feeling that comes over me during biological alteration. I reached up and thought I felt a human eyeball on the back of my head. What was it doing there? Then I became aware of a patch of long human hair growing on my nose. I staggered to the mirror, gazed at my face, and let out a terrified shriek.

23

What I saw in the mirror shocked me to the core.

I was neither human nor alien. I had one human hand and one spiny alien hand. My mouth was red and toothless, and my nose was covered with Zane Tracy hair sprouting all around it. At the end of one leg, I had my alien suction cups. The other leg had a combination of suction cups and three gray, crooked human toes.

Cassidy was staring at me, a look of horror on her face.

"Buddy, what is happening to you?"

"My biological alteration has gone haywire," I said. "I can't control it."

"Try that necklace thing you do."

I reached for the amulet, held it tightly, and chanted.

"*Be Zane. Be Zane now. Pleeaase . . . be Zane now.*"

I felt a flash of current run through my body, and another human eyeball popped out, this one on the top of my bald head.

How I wished I could talk to Grandma Wrinkle. Was this what happens when my alien self ran out of food? Or was something else going on? A sudden and terrifying thought occurred to me. Was my body being controlled by the enemy? Had the Squadron captured Grandma Wrinkle and forced her to destroy my human form?

"Buddy, you have to concentrate," Cassidy said.

"I'm doing the best I . . ."

I couldn't even finish the sentence. I keeled over and collapsed on the carpet. There was a knock on my dressing room door. Cassidy grabbed a blanket off the couch and threw it over me.

"Maybe that's Luis," I said hopefully.

It wasn't Luis. It was Rosa, dropping off my zippered jacket for the red carpet.

"You're all set, Buddy," she said. "Slip this on and get ready for your big night. You need help getting dressed?"

She tried to come in, but Cassidy practically threw herself in front of the door. She took the hanger with my jacket on it and said, "Thanks, Rosa. Buddy will call you if there's a problem."

Rosa craned her neck and tried to get a glimpse inside. She saw me on the floor, but fortunately I was covered up.

"Is he okay?" she asked Cassidy.

"Sure, why do you ask?"

"Um . . . because he's curled up in a ball on the floor."

"Oh . . . that!" Cassidy said. "He's just showing me something he's worked out for a scene in next week's show. You know, the part where the alien curls up into a ball on the floor."

"I didn't see that in the script," Rosa said.

"Yeah, it was just added."

When Rosa left, Cassidy bent down next to me.

"Let me see you," she said.

I held the blanket up to my face. The last thing I wanted was to be seen in this condition. I knew I must look grotesque. Cassidy peeled the blanket off my face.

"How bad is it?" I asked.

"Let me put it this way," she said. "The only fans screaming for you tonight will be the ones that are scared out of their minds."

I rolled over and groaned.

"Can you call Luis and tell him to hurry?" I whispered.

Cassidy took out her phone, and I noticed that her hands were shaking.

"Hello, Luis," she said. "Where are you? Great. Can you walk faster? We really need your guacamole here. Yeah, you might call it that. A guac emergency."

A few minutes later, there was a knock on the door. Cassidy opened it a crack.

"Special delivery from my Grandma Lupe," I heard Luis say. "She gave me every last bit of guacamole she had. Trust me, she's going to have a lot of angry customers tonight."

Cassidy reached out and tried to take four large plastic containers from his hands.

"Thanks, Luis," she said. "We'll call you later."

"Oh no you don't," he said. "I'm coming in. You need to share some of that guacamole."

"No!" Cassidy said. "You can't come in now. Buddy's not feeling well."

"Oh, nerves, huh? Totally understandable."

"Yeah, something like that."

"Well, I've had some experience calming actors down," Luis said. "I have a guided meditation that I do myself, and look how cool I am."

Without taking no for an answer, Luis walked right past Cassidy and came into my dressing room.

"Okay, Buddy, here we go," he said. "Imagine yourself floating on a raft in a tranquil green lake. Hear the birds chirp and the frogs croak."

Luis bent down and started to pull the blanket off my face.

"Don't look, Luis!" Cassidy shrieked.

But Luis went right on. "Your mind is calm as you take in the sights and sounds of nature. Your body is relaxed and—" He stopped suddenly as his eyes took in the sight of me. "HO-LY GUAC-A-MOLE, Buddy!" he screamed. "W-w-what on Earth happened to you?!?!?!"

"I told you not to look," Cassidy said.

Luis's jaw dropped as he looked me up and down, taking in my half-alien, half-human freakish form.

"I hate to get weird, here," he said, his voice shaking. "But something tells me this is not another costume."

"It isn't," I told him. "Can you please pass the guacamole?"

Cassidy took one of the plastic containers, ripped off the lid, and with what strength I had remaining, I grabbed it from her hands. With a *splat*, I practically buried my face in it and wolfed it down. Luis was too stunned to speak.

"More," I croaked.

Luis gave me container number two and I tried to wolf that down too, but I had competition. My sensory enhancer got a whiff of the guacamole and dove for the container, inhaling the spicy green mush with great enthusiasm.

"Give that back," I said, reaching for its snout. "I really need this."

I grabbed hold of my enhancer, trying to wrestle the container away from it. I must have squeezed too hard, because all of a sudden it spit a blob of guacamole directly into my face. I was so desperate, I stuck out both my tongues and wiped my face clean, licking up every last bit. I couldn't afford to miss a drop.

My transformation began almost immediately.

"*Be Zane*," I chanted, grabbing hold of my amulet. "*Be Zane now.*"

I could feel the human eyeball on the top of my head slide down my forehead and land in the proper spot on my face. Then the second human eyeball rotated from the back of my head and took its place next to its partner. The hair covering my nose receded and reappeared on the top of my head.

Luis recoiled like he had seen a monster come alive right in front of him.

"What am I seeing here?" he muttered. "I can't wrap my brain around this."

"I need more guacamole," I said, grabbing the third and fourth containers from his hands. "Do me a favor and hold down my sensory enhancer while I eat this. It's the appendage coming out of my back."

"Dude, are you seriously asking me to touch that thing?" Luis said in horror.

"It's harmless," I said. "It just gets a little carried away around food."

Luis backed away from me and pressed himself against the wall. I continued to struggle with my sensory enhancer and finally managed to subdue it by rolling on my back and pressing hard on the floor to hold it down. Quickly, I gobbled up the rest of the guacamole from containers three and four.

As my body digested the guacamole, it continued to transform. I could feel the human skin as it surrounded me, calming and containing my sensory enhancer. Creeping down my body, the skin covered my legs until my suction cups were completely replaced by my human feet and stubby toes.

"You got some serious explaining to do here, Buddy," Luis said.

I looked over at Cassidy. "I think we have to tell him," she said softly. "It's only fair."

I sighed.

"I really am an alien," I said to Luis. "I come from a red dwarf planet millions of miles from here. I can take a human form, but underneath, I am alien through and through."

Luis was quiet for a long minute. I could see his face twitching, trying to absorb the information I had just laid on him.

"This is all starting to make sense," he said at last. "The costume that you never took off. That's the real you, right?"

I nodded.

"And when you thought pretzels were bracelets? You really didn't know what a pretzel was, did you?"

"No, I didn't."

"And Buddy Cheese Burger, that's not your real name?"

"I saw it on the hamburger stand. My birth name is XR 23 Zeta 5466."

"Wow. Maybe I'll just stick with Buddy."

"Does that mean you'll still be my friend?" I asked him.

I could see that Luis was confused. I couldn't blame him.

What he just witnessed was a lot to digest. He took a long time to answer. "Tell you the truth," he finally said, "it makes me angry that you didn't trust me."

"He couldn't tell you," Cassidy said. "He can't tell anyone. I found out by accident. The bad guys on his planet might be tracking him even at this very moment."

"I do like a good secret," Luis said. "And this one is a secret on steroids."

"I tried to tell you!" I said.

"You were weird from the first moment I met you," Luis said, "but my instinct always told me that you were a cool dude. That hasn't changed."

"Do you have any questions for me?" I asked. "I'll answer anything."

He grinned. "Just one," he said. "Is the limo still coming at six?"

24

I'm happy to tell you that by the time six o'clock came around, all my Zane Tracy parts were arranged in their proper order, and I was feeling strong and fantastically human.

And speaking of fantastic, my first experience on the red carpet was fantastic times a million. Luis, Cassidy, and I rode in a stretch limousine, with neon lights inside that changed color every ten seconds. Delores and Duane and Eloise rode in the limo behind us. I don't mean to brag, but ours was longer.

Our driver opened the sunroof and we stuck our heads out as we drove onto the back lot and passed my spaceship. I'm not sure how many people were on the red carpet because I couldn't see well. Not because my human eyes weren't working—they were in tip-top shape—but because all the cameras were flashing at once.

"Over here, Buddy," the photographers called when I climbed out of the limousine. "Give me a smile."

Cassidy and I walked over to the red carpet, where photographers were lined up behind a rope to get our picture. I was happy to see Ulysses and Martha there, posing and clowning around for the press. The two of them looked really happy. The one who didn't look happy was Tyler. None of the photographers seemed to be calling his name.

I noticed that the reporter Page Robinson was standing next to Tyler, talking on her phone. When she saw me, she dropped her phone in her purse and came running over.

"Buddy!" she said with a grin. "When you're done with the photographers, *Teens Today* is waiting to talk to you live on camera."

Tyler had followed behind her. "What about me?" he asked. "I thought they were supposed to be doing the lead story on me."

"Oh, didn't I tell you?" Page said. "They delayed your story until next week. Seems like our Buddy here has become an overnight Alien Superstar."

"It won't last," Tyler said, giving me a sneer. As he walked away, he added, "Keep your antennas up, doof, because you never know when I'm coming for you."

Past the red carpet in the party area, Luis and Cassidy were having the best time. Cassidy was on the dance floor in her little black dress. At one point, she went to the dessert table, but Delores cut her off before she got there. When Delores wasn't looking, I piled a plate high with chocolaty desserts and brought them to Cassidy. She giggled and ate every single one of them.

"Sorry you can't have these, Buddy," she whispered. "But let's stick with guacamole for the time being. Chocolate makes me break out, but who knows what it would do to you. Maybe you'd turn into a frog and give yourself warts."

On the other side of the dance floor, where buffet tables with silver platters were lined up, Luis was trolling for food. He must have eaten an entire ocean of shrimp, which were being displayed on a table that had a sculpture of a fish chiseled out of a huge block of ice . . .

"This is amazing," he said to me. "Limousines. Live deejays. All the shrimp you can eat. I'm sticking with you, Buddy boy."

Page came to fetch me and brought me to the reporter from *Celebrity Beat*. They had their camera set up next to my spaceship and a bunch of fans were gathered around it.

"We thought this would be a really cute location for your interview," the reporter said. "You know, as if you're a real alien who just flew in on this spaceship."

"That's funny," I said, laughing a little too hard.

The reporter held her mic up to my face.

"Tell me, Buddy, how does it feel going from being a nobody to being a star? Your head must be spinning."

"It's always been a dream of mine," I said.

As I looked into the sky at the stars shining down on us, I realized how true those words were. I had everything I wanted here in front of me. Stardom. Friendships. Fame. Fans. And a TV show right here on Earth. The only thing missing was Grandma Wrinkle. I looked up, half hoping to see a sign from her. And then I saw it, a shooting star traveling across the Hollywood night sky.

No—could it be?

Science told me that it was just a shooting star, but my heart wanted more.

I turned back to the reporter, but as I listened to her next question, something new caught my eye. It was a glowing blue light, pulsating inside my spaceship. Was there someone at the controls? I squinted hard, but I saw no one. Then the light dimmed and disappeared.

I rubbed my eyes. Was that blue glow real or was I just imagining it?

Science told me it was my imagination, but my instincts told me it was a warning sign. But of what?

I turned to my fans and smiled with my best human teeth, but deep inside me, my alien heart was pounding.

THE END

ACKNOWLEDGMENTS

We are grateful to everyone at Abrams Kids, especially our leader, Andrew Smith, our editor, Maggie Lehrman, and the entire Abrams team for helping us bring *Alien Superstar* to life. And of course, we send much respect to our talented illustrator, Ethan Nicolle, who brought Buddy C. Burger and his two worlds into dramatic focus. We are both thankful for our careers in television, especially all the creative talented people who populated our lives on the sound stage. This book is an homage to them.

To our agents, Esther Newberg, Ellen Goldsmith-Vein, and Eddie Gamarra, thank you for being champions of this book, and of all the books we've written together since we started our collaboration. A special thank-you to Theo Baker, our advisor in all things alien. Finally, we thank all of our readers who, since 2003, have supported our vision and shown us their hearts.

Henry Winkler and Lin Oliver
Hollywood, 2019

ABOUT THE AUTHORS

Henry Winkler is an Emmy Award–winning actor, writer, director, and producer who has created some of the most iconic TV roles, including the Fonz in *Happy Days* and Gene Cousineau in *Barry*.

Lin Oliver is a children's book writer and a writer and producer for both TV and film. She is currently the executive director of the Society of Children's Book Writers and Illustrators (SCBWI).

They both live in Los Angeles, California.